SARAH

ANGEL CREEK CHRISTMAS BRIDES BOOK FOUR

PEGGY MCKENZIE

Columbine Publishing Company

*a*ngel Creek, Montana
Christmas Eve 1914

At the well-lived age of seventy-six, Sarah Cassidy rested in her favorite rocking chair in the front parlor that had once been her home. Now it belonged to her daughter, Rebecca, and her family. She was happy to occupy the small bedroom off the kitchen. It was a wonderful place to live out one's life.

Logs in the fireplace blazed hot, but her bones were old. The knitted cover across her lap kept her frail body warm and cozy.

Her longtime friend, Ruby Collins, shuffled into the room from the kitchen and took a seat on the settee. Children of every age sat around the beautiful Christmas tree standing proudly in the big bay window. The children were anxious for the adults to join them.

Several of the younger boys wrestled with each other, unable to contain their excitement. That was the way with boys. And men. They always found a way to test a woman's patience.

Thoughts of her beloved husband, Quinn, settled soft and sweet amidst the children's chatter. Sometimes, when she closed her eyes, she could almost—

"Mother?" Sarah opened her eyes to her daughter's concerned look.

"I'm alright, Becca. I am only resting my eyes for a moment or two."

Her daughter nodded in understanding and planted a tender kiss on her wrinkled cheek. Becca tugged the blanket higher and tucked the corners tight around Sarah's legs. "Mother, the children are settled. They want their Christmas story and it's your turn."

Sarah's gaze fell on every face present. There was so much to be thankful for. Her longtime friends, Julia, Anna, Charity and Ruby were all present along with their children, grandchildren and great grandchildren. The parlor teemed with loved ones.

Someone asked her once if she could have predicted that five, naive young women from Charleston would be so blessed by replying to an advertisement for mail order brides. The answer was always no. She could never have guessed how this great adventure would turn out if she hadn't lived this wonderful life herself.

"Grandma Sarah, tell us how you came to Angel Creek," begged one of her younger great-grandchildren. Sarah thought the girl's name was Lucie, but she couldn't be certain. There were so many children and her mind wasn't as sharp as it once was, but no matter. She loved them all.

Sarah smiled at the little girl who had spoken and pulled her into a hug. "Darling, you have heard me tell this story time and time again. Aren't you tired of hearing it?"

"No, and besides, you and Grandma Charity and

Grandma Julia and Grandma Ruby and Grandma Anna always tell your Christmas stories on Christmas Eve. I want to hear it again." Lucie begged.

"Yeah, we want to hear them again." Charity's great granddaughter, Sarah, chimed in, her little feet dancing with eagerness. Sarah smiled at the child's excitement, honored that one of Charity's great granddaughters was named after her.

Little Sarah slipped her hand into Charity's and sat next to her rocker in the corner by the fire. Sarah observed her friend's eye tear with emotion. She turned to Sarah and smiled encouragement to her. "Go on, Sarah. Tell your story to the children. Tell them why you came to town all those years ago."

Julia grinned and nodded her gray head in encouragement too. "It's a beautiful story worth telling again."

"It's full of love and happiness too," Ruby said, taking her seat to listen.

"That's exactly what I was going to say." Anna said. Sarah cast a fond gaze over her friends and marveled at the fact that she and her friends were still alive and well, still surrounded by the family they loved, and still together. It remained both a blessing and a curse. Thoughts of Quinn resurfaced. Maybe this would be the Christmas—

"Stop woolgathering, Sarah, and tell your story. The children are getting restless." Charity's voice pulled her from her musings.

"Very well." Sarah began the story by rote. It was the same story the five friends told every year on Christmas Eve, ever since that very first Christmas. Each of them told their own tale of heartbreak, desperation, and courage followed by many unexpected blessings.

"The story begins when myself, my daughter, Becca, and my four very best friends in this whole world, left our homes in Charleston to start a new life in a little mountain town called Angel Creek. Montana was still a territory then and we had never seen a wilderness as big as this one.

We arrived just in time too, for there was a most wicked snow storm on the way and us southern girls had never seen anything like it...."

CHAPTER 1

*A*ugust 1865
Charleston, South Carolina

Sarah Caldwell sat ramrod straight in the wingback chair next to the fireplace while her father-in-law paced opposite her. She dug her fingers into her handkerchief hidden between the folds of her dark widow's weeds and twisted it into another knot with each angry step the pompous man took.

She clenched her teeth so tight, the muscles of her cheeks pinched. Somehow, she managed to hold her tongue and wait for him to finish his tirade.

"Sarah, I don't think you are thinking clearly. Since William is dead and can no longer advise you, I think it prudent you should reconsider this ill-advised and rather hasty decision not to take me and Mrs. Caldwell here up on our most generous offer."

Sarah had been raised with impeccable manners, so she

pulled in a deep breath until her corset pinched her ribs and pasted on a smile—of sorts.

"I thank you, Mr. Caldwell. Your offer is appreciated, but Rebecca and I have a home. We would prefer to live among all that is familiar..." Sarah's words trailed off, hating to say the words aloud, "now that my William is gone."

William's father flinched under her words. His fury, fueled by the mention of his only child's name, turned on her. His jowled face splotched with red patches of anger.

"I'll not allow you to speak another word about this subject, Sarah. My decision has been made. You and Rebecca will move into this house immediately." He paused a moment then added. "William would have wanted it that way."

The punch of her father-in-law's words stung as though he had physically attacked her. She sat back in her chair, resentment clawing at her from every quarter of her trembling body. *Stay calm, Sarah. He is using William's name to manipulate you.* She gave herself a moment to breathe. Only then did she contradict her father-in-law's demands.

"Again, I say thank you and I appreciate the offer, Mr. Caldwell. I truly do. But since I am William's widow, shouldn't I be able to make my own decisions about our estate and should not that also include where my daughter and I shall live?"

There. She had finally said what she had been thinking. The outburst of tears from William's mother at the mention of her son's name tore at Sarah's sympathy, but she could clearly see she would not get any support from her mother-in-law. Well, she didn't need their support. *I, too, have made my decision and I will not be bullied as you have done to your son all of his life.*

William's father turned on her once more. This time, there was no pretense of courtesy in his words.

"How dare you contradict my decision. Just because that

weak-spined father of yours allowed you to speak your mind without censure, does not mean you have a voice in making decisions that are clearly out of your authority. A *proper* southern woman would never behave in such a manner to assume she knows more than a man about such matters."

The man intended to stab her with his sharp words, but she didn't care one whit what these people thought. She always knew William's father had little regard for women. Even his own wife he barely seemed to tolerate. Nonetheless, the implication that she'd been raised without proper manners was unacceptable.

"I won't allow you to speak ill of my parents. They are dead and buried, God rest their souls, courtesy of a war whose machinations were started by men like you, Mr. Caldwell. Men who sit and watch the destruction before them with glee, hoping to profit from the lesser man's inability to guide their own destiny.

"My father was a kind and generous man. My mother was beautiful, both inside and out. I never once questioned her love or devotion to me." She fingered her mother's locket hanging from a gold chain around her neck. It was all she had left of her mother.

She shot William's mother a pointed stare hoping the arrow of accusation hit home. Her husband had told her many stories of how he was reared by his nanny, Mrs. Handy, and how his parents would leave home for weeks on end for one reason or another. His mother was always absent, preferring to focus on her social standing rather than the well-being of her only child.

It had sickened Sarah to watch William's mother flit about at parties and prance around like some show pony on his father's arm, moving or talking or sitting at his direction. How dare these pretentious asses speak ill of her parents. Who were these people to judge?

"As God is my witness, Sarah, you will not embarrass the memory of my son any further. Have I made myself clear?" Mr. Caldwell demanded. "Isn't it enough that you are the cause of his death? You killed my son as surely as if you pulled the trigger that fired that fatal bullet into his beating heart."

Sarah almost fainted with shock. William's arrogant ass of a father was blaming her for William's death?

"You cannot be serious, Mr. Caldwell. I begged him not to leave us. He joined a fragmented battalion at the end of a war that was already lost. I pressed him time and time again to explain why he would engage in such a reckless act. His answer was vague and he would only say it was his duty. But his true duty was to remain at home with his wife and child. So, how can you, in all good conscience, find me at fault when I did everything I could to make him stay?"

The man's sneer frightened Sarah. It was a side of her father-in-law she always suspected lay beneath his layers of polished exterior, but she had never witnessed it herself until this moment.

"I find fault because you failed in your duty as my son's wife. You badgered him with your selfish words and accusations of abandonment that made him doubt his decision to go. And it was that doubt that put him in harm's way."

The incredulity of her father-in-law's words punched her in the chest. "How dare you say that to me? If anyone is to blame for my husband's death, it is you, Mr. Caldwell. You pushed your only child into running headlong toward certain death with your talk of duty and honor and other such noble nonsense. Where is your son's honor now, Mr. Caldwell? I'll tell you where it is. It's lying next to him in his grave."

Sarah stood and turned to the door. She had to flee this hellish household of horrors this minute. She passed her mother-in-law's chair and hesitated in mid-step. With measured words, she tried once more to make William's mother see reason.

"I'm sorry, Mrs. Caldwell. I can only imagine how distressing this is for you to hear, but I cannot allow your husband to attack me in such a manner. I will collect my daughter and return to our own home. I'm...sorry things have been so strained between us. William had hoped someday you and I might be friends."

The woman wiped at her tears and looked up at Sarah with red, swollen eyes. The sadness in them tore at Sarah. What it must be like to lose a child—

Sarah was not prepared for her mother-in-law's reaction. Sarah saw the sadness on her mother-in-law's face turn to open hostility. Frances Caldwell raised her cold stare and impaled Sarah's polite control.

"Since we are all speaking our minds this afternoon, Sarah, let me share with you my position on this matter as well. You were William's choice for a wife, but you were never mine. I always thought you unsuitable. And, although you were brought up in a wealthy southern household, that mother and father of yours failed to lead by example. A wife should stand behind her husband, supporting him in his endeavors, not standing in front of him getting in his way." Her words stabbed at Sarah's heart.

She backed away from her mother-in-law's words of disdain. Sarah watched the portly woman stand, using her chair as support until she stood on her own. Sarah had always known her in-laws disapproved of her marriage to William, but she had no inkling as to the extent of their hatred for her until this moment.

"I wish I could say I'm surprised by your words, Mrs. Caldwell, but your behavior toward me these eight years that

I've been married to William has made your feelings quite clear." She refused to play their malevolent game.

Sarah took a moment to calm the irregular beat of her heart before she spoke again. Another breath and her emotions were manageable. She chose to answer her mother-in-law's scorn with an apology or sorts.

"I'm sorry you feel that way, Mrs. Caldwell. I truly am. William and I had hoped, for our daughter's sake, you and I could set our differences aside."

The woman dismissed her words with the flick of her hand. "Don't be ridiculous. You and I were never destined to be friendly. You are not the social climber we had hoped William would marry. You were much too naïve for my son. Why else would the poor boy be forced to seek comfort in the arms of another woman? Caroline Murdoch, now that is the kind of woman I might have befriended. She stole your husband's affections right out from under your trusting little nose.

Sarah's astonishment wheezed through her lungs. "Why would you deliberately parade that woman's name in front of me? She is a conniving female who pretended friendship so she could steal my husband—"

"She didn't steal your husband, Sarah. William was eager to find his pleasures elsewhere and Caroline was waiting."

"William and I were happy," Sarah insisted, though she was not sure whom she was trying to convince of that fact. "We just had a precious baby girl. No, my husband would have never sought out Caroline on his own—" Sarah paused, the truth hitting her square in the face. "You! You are the reason William and Caroline found each other. It was you who pushed them together while I was recovering from childbirth. Do you hate me so much you would sabotage your son's marriage and jeopardize your granddaughter's future?"

"It didn't take much effort, Sarah. Please don't play the victim. It isn't a becoming look on you."

Sarah could take no more. "Please call Mrs. Handy and ask her to bring my daughter down."

But William's mother was not done with her yet. "Ah, that is another matter we must discuss. Rebecca."

"What about my daughter?" Sarah's dread rose, burning and clawing at her stomach. She felt ill.

"As much as I disapproved of your marriage to my son, my disapproval knows no boundaries when it comes to how you teach my only grandchild to be a proper young lady. You allow her too much freedom to do and say as she pleases. And now that William is no longer alive to stay my hand, I can't allow you to continue to parent my granddaughter in this manner."

Sarah repeated the woman's words in her head. *You allow her too much freedom...William can no longer stay my hand...I can't allow you to continue...* What was she alluding to?

Fear clawed at Sarah's throat, making it almost impossible to push the words she needed to say past her lips. She shot a worried glance toward her father-in-law, his smug face making her even more fearful. She recognized the signs of treachery and these two were up to something, of that there was no doubt, and it couldn't be good.

"What do you mean you can't allow me to parent my own daughter? I love my daughter and I will always do what is in Rebecca's best interests. *Always.* How dare you cast aspersions on my ability to raise my child?"

"I dare because I can, Sarah. I dare because Rebecca is *my* granddaughter—my only child's only child and the sole heir to a substantial fortune. I will not allow you to ruin her future. And, without William here to protect his little daughter, she must be guarded from mismanagement."

"Mismanagement? Don't you think that is a strange word

to use when referring to your granddaughter's upbringing?" Sarah armed the statement with as much indictment as possible, and yet her mother-in-law seemed unaffected. The woman continued speaking as if talking about something as mundane as the weather instead of someone she so stridently professed to care about.

"Rebecca will inherit not only the Caldwell fortune but my family's money as well," Mrs. Caldwell told her. "Everything we have will be Rebecca's someday. Surely, even you can see we cannot leave her upbringing to a spineless innocent such as yourself."

Sarah's fear escalated. "Cannot leave her upbringing to her own mother? What choice can you possibly have?"

Mrs. Caldwell walked to stand next to her husband by the fireplace. Sarah recognized the display of solidarity. She had seen it before when they cornered William into doing their bidding against his wishes. The woman's smug expression forewarned Sarah there was more to come. She was not disappointed.

"I had hoped to give you the opportunity to put your daughter's interests above your own selfish ones. However, based upon your decision to refuse our generous and heart-felt offer to allow you to move into our home, you leave us no other alternative but to remove our granddaughter from your custody."

Sarah heard her blood pounding in her ears as the full meaning of William's mother's words punched through the numbness of her shock. "You would take Becca away from me? But, I'm her mother. You—you can't do that. I won't allow it!"

The self-assured air radiating from William's mother guided shivers of dread down Sarah's spine in swelling waves. She held her breath waiting for what would come next.

"You have no say in the matter. We've already spoken to our barrister and he has assured us we have every right to rescue Rebecca." William's mother continued her onslaught of verbal attacks.

" *Rescue her*? From what?" Sarah challenged. "What harm am I causing my daughter?"

"You fail to understand how Charleston works, my dear. Mr. Caldwell and I can well afford to hire any number of witnesses who will attest in a court of law that you are unfit to raise a child of Rebecca's social standing. Since you have chosen to walk your own path by refusing to live with us and accept our guidance in the matter, you leave us no choice but to take Rebecca with us when we leave for Europe this fall. We are closing this house and the house you call home and putting them both up for sale since there is nothing left for us here in Charleston, thanks to this dreadful war."

"You wouldn't do that. Rebecca is my daughter and the house is mine. William left it to me. I am his widow and the mother of his child!" Sarah's courage saddled her indignation and spurred the words out of her mouth with a fury she had never known before. She locked her knees in place and prepared to do battle with these pretentious jackasses.

The smirk on Mrs. Caldwell's lips stretched into a thin, wicked slash across her face. Her words oozed sickly sweet. "Sarah, my dear. I seem to have given you more credit in the intelligence department than you warrant. Surely you cannot be as naive as you are letting on. I shall try to ease your troubled mind and clarify any confusion you are experiencing.

"First, let me assure you, I can do everything I say I can do. Let me explain." The woman's sarcasm dripped from her words as she wandered around the room carelessly touching expensive bric-a-brac as if her words were mundane and unimportant. Sarah knew this conversation was anything but ordinary, and she hung on the harpy's every word.

"The house you currently claim as your own was bequeathed to William from *my* mother when she passed. So, my not-so-clever daughter-in-law, the house and everything in it has been transferred to me upon William's death."

"But—" Sarah's stomach churned in denial. Bile leached into her throat and she nearly choked on her words. "That isn't possible. William wouldn't leave me without—"

"Ahhh, from the look on your poor shattered little face, Sarah, it appears my son has kept that bit of information from you. Now, see what happens when your husband doesn't trust you to have his best interests at heart?"

Sarah thought back over the weeks before William left home. "I don't believe you. William would never have gone to war knowing there was a possibility he wouldn't return and leave me without means to support myself. He...he wouldn't do that." Sarah's words fell into troubled silence. Doubt clouded her thoughts and she searched for a contradiction to this madness within the snippets of conversations she'd had with William about this very subject.

"Oh, my dear. He has done just that. He has always known if something happened to him, the estate would be mine."

Sarah's thoughts reeled. How could this be true? Had William betrayed her and their daughter by leaving them penniless and at the mercy of his parents he knew to be unyielding and heartless? *Oh, William. How could you?* She had to seek advice from a counsellor. Immediately.

"I see by the panic on your face you realize what I am saying is true," Mrs. Caldwell gloated.

Sarah refused to give up her daughter without a fight. "I think we understand each other. Now, please ask Mrs. Handy to bring my daughter down. We have much to do today." Sarah slipped on her gloves and threw her lightweight cape around her shoulders.

"I think you shall be sorely disappointed, Sarah." Mrs.

Caldwell called out. "Mrs. Handy, please bring Rebecca into the parlor. Her mother wishes to say goodbye."

Out of the corner of Sarah's eye, she caught a movement. William's aged childhood nanny stood in the doorway holding Becca's hand. The woman must have been standing in the hallway waiting for her employer's summons. Had her daughter overheard the exchange between her mother and her grandparents? Dear God, she hoped not. Becca was much too young to understand such nonsense.

"Come Becca. Let's go. We have much to do." Sarah rushed to her daughter, intent on getting her out of this madhouse as soon as humanly possible. But when she approached Becca, she stepped behind Mrs. Handy and clung to the woman's long skirt.

"Becca, honey. Come to Mommy." Her daughter shook her head in refusal. "Please, Rebecca. Take my hand. We have to go home right away." Again, her daughter refused.

Sarah turned an accusatory stare at her in-laws. William's mother shrugged as though she had no clue at all what the matter was. Sarah knew better.

Becca's sweet little face crumbled. Her little girl's sobs shredded Sarah's heart. She reached out for her again, but this time, Becca screamed at her in red-faced anger amidst her tears. "Grandmother said you killed my daddy! I hate you!"

Sarah stared in disbelief while her six-year-old daughter raced up the legendary Caldwell staircase and disappeared over the second story landing. Mrs. Handy sent her a sympathetic shrug and followed Becca up the stairs.

Sarah turned on her in-laws, clenching her fists in rage. "You told my daughter I killed her father? What kind of monsters are you?"

Her contemptible father-in-law sauntered to the sideboard and poured himself a glass of whiskey from one of the crystal containers lining the top of the liquor cabinet. He swirled the amber colored liquid in the glass and tossed it down his throat.

She tried not to raise her voice. She truly did, but she was in a nightmare spiraling out of control. "I asked you a question," she demanded. "Why would you tell Becca that I killed her father knowing full well it isn't true?"

Instead of answering her question, William's father called out to his manservant hovering just out of sight, "Jeffrey, will you show Sarah to the door?"

The man appeared instantly and stood aside, signaling that Sarah should follow. Sarah was at an impasse. She had no choice but to retreat and regroup for the battle that was coming.

"Very well. I will go. For now." She emphasized her words with a pointed stare to both of William's smug, sadistic parents. "But understand this, I am your son's widow and there is nothing you can do to change that without jeopardizing Becca's rights as his daughter. And if you think for one moment I'm going to allow you to abduct my daughter without retribution, you have another think coming to you."

Sarah spun on her heels and fled from the parlor without waiting on Jeffrey to open the twelve-foot solid cypress door. She gripped the brass handle and, with every ounce of strength she possessed, slung it wide open, sending it slamming against the wall with a satisfying crash. She heard the sound of glass breaking against the tile floor behind her and she prayed it was a most prized possession—and very, *very* expensive.

She stomped down the sidewalks of Charleston's finest neighborhood, the oppressive heat of the muggy afternoon in August sending beads of perspiration to bubble and run underneath her smothering crinolines.

Beyond the sight of William's despicable parents, she

stopped and glared at the clear cloudless sky and shook her fist.

"William, I swear to you, as God is my witness, I will not allow your sadistic parents to play these emotional games with Rebecca. *They* are the ones that sent you to an early grave with their false words of honor and loyalty." Tears burned her eyes and a single tear slipped down her cheek. She flicked it away with an impatient finger and set her determination firmly in place. "There will be no more tears on your behalf, husband. You betrayed me, William. With Caroline. With your parents. With the truth of your estate. Every time you had a choice to make, you never chose me. You never once chose me."

Sarah shoved her grief down deep inside her gut and shot another fuming glare toward the heavens. Her attention now focused on the matter at hand. She needed a plan. Any plan that would help her keep Becca out of the Caldwells' reach. Her determination to protect her child knew no boundaries.

She gathered her courage and turned down the hot steamy sidewalk toward the home she no longer had a right to live in. She mumbled under her breath. "I will go anywhere, do anything, to save my daughter from the cruelty of your parents' tainted love, William. And I do mean *anything.*"

CHAPTER 2

*a*ngel Creek, Montana Territory
Mid-November 1865

Sarah Caldwell stepped from the stage coach, alongside her friends and her daughter, into the chilling November wind.

The mountains behind her and the beautiful forest of pines surrounding her did nothing to quell her nervous expectation of being followed. She hadn't witnessed any signs of pursuit during the steam boat ride from St. Louis, but one could never be too certain of anything where the Caldwells were concerned.

The trip from Charleston to the trading post on the Missouri River had been as comfortable as one could expect on a boat this time of year. She was glad to have her true friends, women who really cared about her and her daughter, along for support.

Conversations with Charity, Julia, Anna, and Ruby indicated they were as full of conflicting emotions as she about becoming mail order brides to total strangers. Never in her wildest dreams would she have considered so bold a plan. But then, she had never been put into such a position before. Her daughter's safety came above all other considerations. William's ruthless parents left her no choice.

The stage coach ride from the trading post hadn't taken more than a few hours, and she was ever so grateful. The vast emptiness of this wilderness was unlike anything she had seen before. It frightened her. Life in a bustling city taught her help was only the bat of an eyelash away. That would not be the case in this isolated country.

A wolf's howl somewhere in the distance sent a shiver of fear through her body. Goosebumps pimpled her skin underneath her many layers of heavy wool. She pulled her cloak closer around her throat and cast a nervous glance over her shoulder once more.

"Will you relax, Sarah? You're free now. There is no way your in-laws can find you all the way in Montana. No way at all. Especially after you're married and change your name," Charity assured her.

Sarah wanted to believe her friend, but she knew what William's parents were capable of and she could only imagine how they reacted to the realization she had stolen Becca right out from under their self-righteous noses. She hoped Mrs. Handy didn't suffer the wrath of their unreasonable fury. It wasn't the poor woman's fault Sarah took Rebecca in the middle of the night. She was quite proud of her success. That would teach those people to underestimate a naïve young woman with a brain.

"I hope so, Charity," Sarah said. "I truly do, but I can ill afford to underestimate the Caldwells. They have unlimited resources to track me down if they so desire. And I am very much afraid they will stop at nothing to have Becca back under their control as she is their only heir. And having me thrown in jail to rot would give their black hearts much delight, I fear."

"Well, it's too late to turn back now. We're to be married as soon as we arrive and, as you can see, we have arrived." Charity's words reminded Sarah of the seriousness of this decision. Doubts swirled inside her chest once more.

"Yes, we most assuredly are here." Sarah shivered again under the damp, cold air. She pulled her heavy woolen cloak tighter once more and watched a few gigantic snowflakes settle, soft and quiet, one on top of another. Sarah was so grateful they arrived when they did. The sky looked dark and ominous. She hoped it was not a harbinger of things to come.

Would she get used to this bone-chilling cold after living in Charleston her whole life? She wished it to be so. Lucky for her, she had managed to horde her weekly allowance from William's barrister before the Caldwells put a stop to it. And when she and her friends decided to accept the mail order bride proposals, she spent almost every penny—except for one $20 gold piece tucked safely into her corset—on warm clothing, socks and boots for her and Becca.

"Momma, I hate it here. It's too cold. My toes are freezing. Can't we go back to Grandmother's? I don't understand why we had to come here. I miss my friends. I miss Mrs. Handy. I miss my pony, Eleanor, and I miss my dog, Annabelle."

Sarah's stomach pitched at her daughter's complaints. Her in-laws had stopped at nothing to buy her daughter's love in the three months they held her hostage. Sarah hadn't been allowed to see her but twice, and that was due to the generosity of Mrs. Handy, William's aged nanny.

She supposed the woman still had some decency despite living in that hellish household. Or perhaps it was because she lived in that household she took pity on Sarah. Whatever the reason, the woman had risked incredible retribution by allowing her to see her daughter. She would be forever grateful to the elderly nanny. And unbeknownst to the woman, she gave Sarah the perfect opportunity to plan her daughter's escape.

"I know you miss them, sweetheart, but this is where we live now. Isn't it beautiful?" Sarah encouraged her daughter to see the beauty of their new surroundings. She took Becca's little hand and walked toward the church with her friends.

Becca was not going to make this transition easy for any of them. She had spent the entire trip complaining to Sarah and demanding to go back to see her friends. But there was no going back for any of them now. Moving toward an uncertain future was the only option available to them.

She pulled her daughter along beside her, taking care to point at the pretty trees and falling snowflakes. Snow never fell in Charleston, so under other less confusing circumstances, the sight would have been a delightful treat.

She understood Becca's confusion. One day she had been a happy, carefree six-year-old girl with nothing on her mind except which dress to choose for her best friend's birthday party or riding her pony or playing with her dog. Then, suddenly, she was knocked off her feet with the news her beloved father had been killed and would never be coming home—not ever again.

The people who were supposed to be doting grandparents and want only the best for her, told her horrible, vicious lies about her mother. And then the mother she believed to be responsible for her father's death stole her away from everything she loved.

Sarah understood the gut-wrenching emotions her little girl was feeling. She dealt with them no less herself. However, Becca's frequent outbursts—repeating the Caldwells' lies in public—would make them more vulnerable to discovery if William's parents were in pursuit. Her instincts told her she and her friends had left a trail a mile wide even a blind coon dog could follow, and the Caldwell's money would buy someone much more experienced and determined than a blind coon dog.

"Come on, someone is calling to us from the church door," Charity called out.

Sarah was about to meet her new groom. A stranger. And, she was to be married. *To. Be. Married. Ugh. Another husband.* Was there no destiny available to a woman that did not include a keeper masquerading under the guise of a husband?

When she married William, she thought they would spend their days filled with happiness and love. She rolled her eyes heavenward and wished for the independence of her youth.

Sadness stabbed at her heart when she thought of the day she got the news she had lost her parents and Edgewood, the sprawling estate she called home. Yankee soldiers had appeared from nowhere, burned everything, then disappeared back into the shadows. Her memories and her loved ones were stolen in an instant by flames set to pass judgement for sins not understood.

Sarah and her friends arrived at the church door. A thin elderly man who introduced himself as Henry waited for them at the top of the stairs and ushered them inside.

"Oh, what a beautiful place." Sarah marveled at the carved pine pews lining the sanctuary. The two rows of benches allowed for a wide center aisle. Stained-glass windows formed a mosaic of beautiful colors set between lines of leaded cane. Even the dim light of the gray, cloudy day filtered through the windows as little rainbow-colored prisms of light. She was amazed something this beautiful could exist out here in such a wild country.

"It's a lovely sanctuary," Charity whispered. "Much nicer than I thought it would be."

The man called Henry led them down the aisle to the front of the church. He extended his arm to the front pew. "Have a seat here. Reverend Tilly arrives in a few moments."

Sarah noticed a group of men standing on the opposite side of the church near the open fireplace. Ruby whispered, "I wonder which one belongs to which of us."

Becca fidgeted in the seat next to her. "Momma. I'm tired. I wanna go to sleep."

"I'm sorry, Becca. I know you are tired. We all are. Please be patient, sweetheart. And keep your voice down. You are in church."

Sarah whispered back to Ruby over Becca's head. "I was just wondering the same thing myself." She cut a glance toward the group of men to take another peek, but she was careful not to appear as though she were taking another look. "A lady must never appear too eager," her mother always told her.

She stole a discreet glance here and there hoping to determine which one she was going to wed. Her nerves were on edge. She rubbed her gloved hands together, hoping to dispel some of her anxiety. Anna sat up straight. "Wait, there's only four of them. Shouldn't there be five?"

Sarah cut her eyes toward the group of men to take another look. To Anna's credit, there were only four. Her heart sank to the bottom of her snow-soaked stockings. What if her groom had changed his mind? What would happen to her and Becca then? Stunned at the possibility, she openly stared at the group of men, observing them one by one. Which one could be missing?

"Momma. I said I'm tired. And I'm hungry. When are we going to eat?"

"Soon, honey. Please be patient. Here, play with this hymnal. See if you can read any of the words." Sarah handed the book to her daughter and turned her attention back to the group of men. Three men were facing toward her talking to the fourth groom who had his back to her. One of the men caught her gaze and nodded. She turned away, embarrassed to have been caught studying the men.

Charity smiled and nodded to the group then whispered to her and Julia. "They are all so handsome. It's impossible to tell which one belongs to which of us."

Hadn't any of the men described themselves in their letters? Sarah wondered. Had she told her groom-to-be what she looked like? She honestly couldn't remember. It hadn't seemed important at the time. All she desired was to escape Charleston, and her treacherous in-laws with her daughter.

Think, Sarah. What did his letters say? She closed her eyes trying to see the letter with her mind's eye and find some clue as to which one of the men might be her new husband.

Sarah thought hard. She couldn't remember. She found the fact that she didn't know what her groom looked like quite curious. And disturbing.

Suddenly, it came to her. "Wait. I do remember something." Her friends all looked at her in anticipation. "My groom, Quinn Cassidy, said he was clean shaven. He said he didn't like the scratch of a beard on his face."

All five women turned their heads toward the group of men. Anna stated the obvious. "Well, the three men facing us have beards, so it could be the one with his back to us belongs to you, Sarah."

"Just my luck. Or, it could be the one missing that belongs to me." She admitted her concern. "What will I do if my groom doesn't show up?"

"Focus on the positive, Sarah. Was there anything else that could identify your groom?" Charity asked.

Sarah thought about the letters again. Her mind's eye scanned the neat script slanted across the pages. "Wait, yes. I do remember something else. Mr. Cassidy said he had a scar on his cheek."

"Which cheek?" Charity asked eyeing the men in the corner.

Sarah couldn't remember. "I honestly don't know."

"I said I'm hungry and I want to go to bed!" Becca threw the hymnal to the hardwood floor. The shocking crash disrupted the silence of the church and echoed off the white-washed walls.

Sarah was mortified. She shot an embarrassed look toward the men. Every one of them had turned their attention to the book on the floor, including the one with the clean-shaven face. The one with the jagged white scar on his left jawbone. The one—with the shiny sheriff's star pinned to his vest.

Stunned, Sarah picked up the hymnal off the floor and hugged it to her breasts while she slumped against the hard back of the wooden pew. She heard a voice admonish Becca for her inappropriate behavior. Charity? Anna? Julia perhaps. She couldn't be sure. Her mind was a muddled mess of hope and fear fighting with each other to maintain control.

She should have been relieved to learn her new husband-to-be was a very handsome man. And she should have been delighted he hadn't run from the church when he witnessed Becca's tantrum. She should have been grateful. Instead, she was terrified. Why hadn't she known she had accepted the proposal of a lawman? Could a husband arrest his wife in Montana Territory? She had no idea.

Dear God, what have I done?

Quinton Cassidy was as nervous as a colt in a corral full of wolves. He admitted he'd agreed to this little venture of ordering a wife through an advertisement, but he wasn't certain the reality was as logical as the original idea had been.

The women from Charleston had arrived a few moments ago. All five ladies and the one little girl sat on the front pew opposite from where he and his co-groomsmen stood. He observed them walk down the center aisle of the church single file and take the seats offered on the front pew.

Every one of them was a real beauty. He was surprised these women from Charleston were so breathtaking.

He turned to steal another glance at the dark-haired woman who sat next to the little girl. The church was small and made it easy to hear their whispers to each other. They were as curious about their grooms as he and his friends were about their brides.

It was the dark-haired woman who declared her groom was clean shaven. That could only mean him, since practically every other man in Angel Creek grew a beard for protection against the frigid Montana Territory winters.

His heart stuttered. So, this was the beauty who had agreed to be his wife. *Sarah*. He liked her name. And the little girl next to her was to be his daughter. Her coloring was so different than her mother's. The golden blond hair and light blue eyes must have come from the little girl's father.

A twinge of guilt poked Quinn's chest. He agreed to this mail order marriage because he needed a wife—*wanted a wife*. But, when he learned that one of the women was a confederate soldier's widow with an orphan in tow, he wondered if this woman's husband—the little girl's father—had been one of the many casualties in grey he was responsible for before he himself had almost been killed.

He questioned the man at the newspaper who published the advertisement for the mail order brides. He asked if there was more information about the woman and her past. It was a big relief to learn the woman's husband had died just this last spring—long after Quinn was wounded and discharged from service in the fall of '63. The last thing he wanted to do was start a marriage with the widow of a soldier he encountered on the battlefield.

He pushed the morbid thought out of his mind. This was his chance to repay at least one of those fallen men who had been taken from their families. He would vow to love, honor and cherish his enemy's wife and child in hopes of some small measure of redemption for his part in that hellish war.

The Reverend Tilly entered from a side door and walked to the pulpit. "Gentlemen, please step this way and let's get everyone acquainted with each other before we begin the ceremony, shall we?"

Quinn followed his fellow groomsmen, Lewis Huntington, Matthew Bailey, and Trevor Collins to stand in front of the reverend, shoulder to shoulder. He hadn't known Lewis long, but he seemed like a good man. Trevor was the town's doctor who cared for his community. And Matt, that man worked his tail off on his ranch just outside of town. Then there was Levi Steele, another rancher that lived out of town —*wait a minute.*

He leaned over to Lewis and whispered. "Where's Levi?"

Lewis shrugged and shook his head. "I have no idea. He said he'd be here on time."

Reverend Tilly cleared his throat and smiled at everyone. "Ladies, could you please come forward and I'll introduce you to your grooms. I trust everyone here is ready to be married." Quinn felt the awkward silence that followed the reverend's attempt at humor.

"Levi isn't here yet," Quinn offered, unsure what he could do if the man had changed his mind about being married today.

The reverend's face flushed, and he cleared his throat

again. "I see. Well, I suppose we can wait a few moments for him, considering there is a storm brewing, but I think it prudent we don't delay too long since some of you live outside of town."

The reverend motioned for the ladies from Charleston to join their grooms.

Quinn watched his bride, holding her daughter's hand, come to stand beside him. Her eyes never met his. Did that mean she was embarrassed, bashful, or avoiding him? That thought punched him in the gut. What if his beautiful new wife didn't like the way he looked? He stroked his face touching the scar on his cheek with his thumb.

The door to the chapel opened and banged shut. Everyone turned to see Levi Steele, striding down the aisle. His dirty clothing and boots indicated he had rode hard to get here.

His friend sent a look of apology to everyone and walked to the front of the room to stand next to Trevor. "I'm sorry, everyone. I had a hell—um, sorry Reverend— I had a *heck* of a time getting to town today. Preparations for my livestock ahead of this storm and then on the way to town, I—" Levi stopped short. "Sorry. I'll shut up now."

"Very well, then." The reverend nodded to everyone. "Now that all of our grooms are present and accounted for, gentlemen, please take your bride's hand in yours and repeat after me."

Quinn turned to the dark-haired woman next to him and took her small hand into his. She was shaking. Nerves? He didn't blame her. He was a bit shaky himself. They were strangers about to pledge the rest of their lives to one another.

The Reverend Tilly's voice forced him to pay attention. "Grooms. Please repeat after me. I, your name, take thee, your bride's name, to be my wedded wife, to have and to hold, from this day forward.

The enormity of what he was about to do hit home with a good solid punch to his gut.

Dear God, what have I done?

CHAPTER 3

*S*arah looked around the pitiful interior of the sheriff's home and cringed. It was the size of her summer kitchen back home. How on earth were three people supposed to live in such a tiny place?

Her attention was pulled to the sound of the shrill tune of a piano playing raucous music from the saloon across the street. Charity was now married to the saloon owner. Lewis-something. Her friend was going to live inside that den of immoral women and ungodly men. How had she and her friends fallen so far from grace? This move, these marriages —it was all supposed to be the answer to their prayers, but how could it be possible—

"Ma'am? Did you hear what I said?"

The sheriff—her *husband* was speaking to her. She turned to him trying not to appear befuddled. "I'm sorry. I—what was that you said, Mr. Cassidy?"

The tall, handsome man smiled in understanding. "Please. Call me Quinn. I said I am fully aware this isn't what you're used to." His apologetic gaze wandered around the room. "To be honest, I've never really looked at this old place through anyone else's eyes but my own."

She didn't contradict him. She couldn't. What could she say? *I'm used to living in a mansion where my clothing has more room than this.*

"When I rented it from the previous owner, I just needed it for a place to sleep. Sometimes I cooked, but usually I ate at Mr. Oliver's restaurant. We have a lot to figure out, don't we? In the meantime, you can put your things anywhere you like. This is your home now, yours and Rebecca's." He nodded to her daughter, who was peering out the window at the saloon across the street. "And you can do with it what you will."

She acknowledged his offer with a nod because she had no words at the moment.

"Momma, where is my room? I don't like it here. I want to go back to grandmother's house." Becca's high-pitched demands managed to overcome the garish music from across the street sending a spike of pain into Sarah's throbbing head. This situation was unbearable. What had she been thinking? She fingered her mother's locket for courage. It was a reminder of the past she longed to return to.

The sheriff smiled and offered her daughter a suggestion. "Rebecca, this old house has a little room off the back of the kitchen where I keep some odds and ends. It's big enough to fix up into your own special room. If you want it, it's yours."

Becca screamed at the sheriff's offer. "I don't want a room here. I want to go home!"

Mr. Cassidy looked a bit flummoxed at Becca's outburst and Sarah was mortified. She wanted to go home too. But there was no longer a home to go to. There was no future for her back in Charleston. There was only a probable jail cell waiting for her. And Becca? William's parents would steal her away to Europe and she would never lay eyes on her precious daughter again.

Hat in his hand, her new husband squatted down to Becca's level. "I understand this place isn't what you're used to either, Miss Rebecca, but in time, your momma will make this ole' place shine like a diamond in a goat's as—" Quinn stopped short and cut an embarrassed look in her direction. "Uh, sorry. I'm not used to having to watch my language around little girls. Or full-grown women, for that matter. I've spent most of my time around men. And horses."

Sarah's regard for the man increased tenfold at his kind consideration of her daughter's innocence. "Thank you, Sheriff. I appreciate your effort in deportment."

"Again, the name is Quinn. I'd appreciate it if you called me by my name. Sheriff doesn't seem right. For a wife to call her husband, that is." Awkward silence followed when she didn't answer. She finally managed to nod in agreement. *Quinn* continued. "And your name is Sarah if I'm remembering correctly. "

She tried to relax. "Yes, Sarah is correct. And you may call me, well, Sarah. I suppose." She was at a loss as to how to act around this stranger that was now her new husband. She fumbled with her reticule cords and looked everywhere but at him.

He laughed, a deep throaty sound that pulled her gaze back to his handsome face. Her breath caught, and she surprised herself when she smiled back. "That sounded silly even to my own ears." She offered in explanation.

"Not silly at all. Sounds like a practical woman to me."

His unexpected compliment sent a wave of delight to her scarred and disappointed heart. She hadn't known joy in such a long time, the sensation caught her off guard. And to have another human being besides her parents pay a compliment to her intelligence instead of how she looked, well, it was quite uplifting.

"Momma! I said I wanna go home!" Becca's shriek poked

at Sarah's momentary happiness. Her daughter stomped a booted foot on the bare wood floor. Sarah knew she needed to discipline her daughter, but her child had been through so much these past few months. There would be time for that sort of thing later, when Becca was more settled. Thoughts of her mother-in-law's disdain for her parenting skills punched at her courage so she dismissed them. She needed every ounce of courage she had at the moment.

Her husband stood. "Um, well I hate to leave you alone on your first night in town," Quinn told her, his frown full of regret. "But I do have a job to do. The U.S. Marshall from Great Falls delivered a prisoner here today. He's sending a prison wagon to pick him up in a day or so. Trouble is, with this storm, it's gonna depend on how much snow falls whether that heavy iron wagon can get through the passes. I hope sooner rather than later, that's for sure."

Sarah watched the sheriff cut his glance toward Becca. "So, I'll give you two lovely ladies time to settle in. I hired a neighbor lady to come in and clean the place up, change the bed sheets, that sort of thing. There's water in the pitcher on the table next to the bed for washing up tonight. Tomorrow, I'll work on getting that bath tub off the back of the house and settin' it up for you in here where it's warm if you have a mind to take a bath instead of a wash from the basin. I'd offer to send you to the bath house but that wouldn't be the kind of place for a lady and a little girl. Mostly saddle tramps and soldiers riding through stop there, so—"

Quinn slipped his arms into his coat and reached for his hat on the seat of the lone rocking chair in the room. "I'll be back at first light since I have to stand guard tonight. Tomorrow, I'll hire a deputy, so I won't have to be on duty all the time—now that I have a family and all."

He nodded and started to leave when she saw him hesitate again. Then he walked to her pouting daughter, Becca's arms crossed over her chest in defiance. Quinn knelt in front of her rebellious child and said, "Miss Rebecca, I know this move to Angel Creek can't be easy for you. Or your momma. You had a good life back in Charleston, and for whatever reason you had to leave your friends and all your things—"

"And my pony Eleanor and my dog Annabelle too. They miss me," Becca pointed out.

"Yes, I'm sure they do miss you. A lot. And I'm sure it isn't easy on you, being without your pony and dog either."

Sarah could see her daughter struggle with the unexpected kindness of this stranger.

"I also want you to understand how sorry I am about the loss of your father. I won't even try to tell you that I'm gonna make all this better. Nobody can take his place because he was a special man and I could never ever be as good a father to you as he was."

Her daughter's bottom lip trembled, and Sarah saw the glint of tears pooling in Becca's crystal blue eyes. Sarah was having a hard time stemming her own tears at the man's heartfelt words.

"But I also want you to remember this, when I married your momma, I married you too. And I will do the best job I can to take care of you and to love you and provide for you. And that is a promise from my heart to yours." Quinn pointed from his chest to Becca's when he said the words.

Her daughter's angry face crumbled with emotion. Tears streamed down her little cheeks and she ran from the room into the only bedroom and slammed the door behind her. Her sobs could be heard even through the closed door.

The expression on Quinn's face tore at Sarah's heart. He stood and twirled his hat in his hand. "I'm sorry—I thought I was trying to reassure her, but I guess I messed up already. This father thing is new to me."

A single tear slipped down her own cheek and she swiped

it away. "It's not your fault, Mr. Cassidy. I mean Quinn. Really. It isn't. She's been through a lot for a little girl her age and she's lost so much. Perhaps, we all just need a little time to adjust. That's all."

The man she now called husband nodded his understanding. "I get it. And this place isn't exactly a palace."

Sarah couldn't argue that point, but she wanted to offer him something in return for all he was doing for her and her daughter. "Well, perhaps not at the moment, but there is something to be said for starting from scratch, isn't there?" She mustered as much enthusiasm as she was able, standing in the midst of a sad little room in the center of a sad little house.

He looked around the room for a moment and then his warm, golden eyes settled back on her. "I suppose that is one opinion on the condition of this old place. Well, anyway, I've got money in the bank and I receive a monthly pension from my military retirement. You are welcome to it, so you can, you know, fix this place up. Make it seem like more of a home for Becca." He quickly added, "And you, of course."

Sarah was touched by the man's generosity. William never allowed her access to his money. He gave her an allowance and made her account for every penny at the end of each week. It suddenly dawned on her that Quinn said he had a military pension. That meant he was a soldier. Maybe he knew William.

"You are a retired soldier? Perhaps you knew my husband. He was a member of the 6th South Carolina Cavalry Regiment. His name was William Caldwell. Do you have knowledge of him?" Sarah hoped he did. She would love to hear him regale Becca with stories about William. She was sure her daughter would love it even more.

"No, ma'am. I wouldn't have been acquainted with your husband. You see...I was an officer on the side of the Union."

35

Sarah's ears started to ring. Her breath left her body and she couldn't seem to pull any back into her lungs. The tin paneled ceiling tilted at an odd angle and Sarah felt herself falling. Strong arms caught her and carried her to the single rocking chair in the center of the room.

Air forced its way back into her lungs and her vision cleared. She heard a man's voice call to her from some great distance.

Quinn squatted in front of her. "Sarah, are you alright?" His worried face stared up at her.

She looked into his eyes a moment or two longer. Just a few moments ago, this man had touched her to her core with his kindness to her and her daughter. But now, all she could think about was—

"Sarah? Talk to me. Are you okay? Is something wrong?"

"Yes, *Mr.* Cassidy. Something is very wrong. My late husband, and the father of my only child, is dead and buried —and my whole life has changed in a most devastating manner, because of men like you!"

Quinn walked the short distance to his office in a daze. *What the hell just happened?* He peeked in on the federal prisoner called Little Johnny Bishop in one of the four barred cells in the back room of his jail.

"Hey, when am I gonna get some food?" The man demanded.

"Shut up and go to sleep. It's getting' late." Quinn advised the man. He was in no mood for a bunch of—

"Damn, Sheriff. What burr stuck under yer saddle? I ain't been here long enough for ya to be mad at me." Little Johnny had a peculiar accent Quinn couldn't place.

The prisoner walked over to the single hay-padded cot

and sat. He smirked at Quinn. "Must be woman troubles. I hope that don't mean I'm gonna miss my suppa. Mawshall said youse was gonna bring me my suppa."

Quinn turned the iron key in the lock and grunted toward his prisoner. His irritation hitched up another notch. The man hit a little too close to home with his guess.

"Don't you worry about eatin', Mr. Bishop. You'll eat dinner when it gets here. Now stop talking and go to sleep. It's late. You should have been here hours ago." Quinn wanted to be mad at somebody. Might as well be this sorry excuse for a human being whose crime was robbin' banks and putting law abiding citizens at risk.

"The storm slowed us down, Sheriff. Couldn't be hepped." Quinn wondered where that accent was from, but right now he didn't have time to worry over it. He had a whole passel of problems of his own to ponder a solution before mornin'.

Quinn slammed the wooden door between his office and the cells to shut out the yells of his new prisoner. He'd feed him alright, but not until he got good and ready. And right now, he wasn't ready.

He had sent the federal marshal down the street to the hotel for a bite to eat and some rest to wait for the storm to pass. The man looked dog tired and he had a long ride at first light if the snow didn't get too deep for him to ride out.

Quinn might as well get comfortable. It was gonna be a long night sitting in his hard bow-backed office chair. He thought back over the last few hours. His plans to help a confederate widow and her daughter had taken a serious turn for the ditch. How could this woman be so offended that he'd fought for the Union? He hadn't killed her husband. He had made certain of that. He had already been discharged from the Union Army because of his own injuries by the time her husband was killed.

Perhaps she should realize those same men she championed were the same ones who inflicted these horrific injuries on him. They did their best to send him to the hereafter, and they almost succeeded. He cringed at the memories.

He thought about the white cords of scars on his stomach and left thigh. It was a damn Rebel ball that almost took his life. It sure as hell took away his ability to ever father a child, at least that was the final report of his surgeon after he woke from surgery.

That was another reason he chose this woman to marry. Her daughter would be the only one he would ever have the privilege to father, but the way things were lookin', takin' a mail order bride sight unseen may not have been his best idea. He needed to talk to his fellow groomsmen. He hoped they were faring better than he was with their new brides.

Now that he thought about it, he should have raised a couple of questions to her in his letters before he asked for her hand in marriage. He never thought for one moment she would be so narrow-minded as to hold a single man responsible for the whole damned war. He sure as hell didn't hold her personally liable for all the men he lost under his command. He was following orders just like every other poor soul sucked into that hellish—

Enough.

He pulled his hat off his head and jabbed it on the coat rack next to the front door of his office. His wet heavy canvas coat followed.

Quinn's boots scraped across the rough wooden floor. He opened the side door leading to the alley between the jail and the apothecary building next door and pulled four logs from the wood rack nailed to the wall just outside.

A quick glance around his surroundings and he knew winter had arrived in Angel Creek. Darkness had fallen and the early winter storm chilled the damp air. Snowflakes the size of saucers floated from a gray winter sky and lined the frozen mud-lined streets of town.

A small shiver pushed him back inside and Quinn closed the side door against the cold. The iron door of the pot-bellied stove in the corner groaned in protest when he shoved the sticks of wood inside. He stirred the shimmering coals to life with the iron poker hanging on the side of the stove and slammed the door closed. Embers in the stove roared to life. The flames ignited, consuming the dry wood amidst crackles and pops.

Quinn pulled in a satisfied sigh and walked to one of the windows that bookended the heavy wooden front door of his office. He drew back the curtain to reveal gold lettering across the window. *Sheriff's Office*. He knew behind the other window curtain was a single gold star representing the badge he wore on his chest. A sense of pride came with wearing that tin star and in a job well done protecting the citizens of this remote wilderness town.

A peek outside into the darkness revealed empty streets with only a few lonely souls—who had no one waiting for them at home—huddled against the icy precipitation falling from a heavy sky. He thought once he got married, all that would change for him. Matt and Trevor had shared much the same sentiments when they agreed to pursue wives through an advertisement. Again, he wondered if they were having better luck than he was settling their new families. He sure hoped so.

He took another look through the window. The snow was really coming down hard now. Quinn was glad the women arrived when they did. Otherwise, they would have either been stranded on the trail between town and the riverboat trading post or they would have had to remain another week or so aboard the steamer. He wondered about

39

one particular dark-haired woman just three doors down from where he paced. A very angry dark-haired woman.

Perhaps he had been naive in dismissing how deep those feelings of hatred were between the two sides. What on earth had possessed him to agree to marry a stranger—especially a confederate stranger? *Loneliness.*

Quinn shook off his morbid thoughts for the moment. Nothing he could do to fix the problem right this minute and besides, he had a job to do.

He peeked out the window and down the street toward the saloon. Lewis was really packin' 'em in tonight. All the windows of the saloon were ablaze with lights. Did that mean his friend, Lewis, had to leave his bride to sleep alone too? He watched shadowed silhouettes dance back and forth across the lighted windows. *At least someone was having fun.*

Quinn cut a quick glance behind him to the door that separated his office from the prisoner cells. He would have to open that door tonight and let the warmth of the fire in his office reach the man in the cell. His reputation as a lawman wouldn't fair too well if his allowed the man to freeze to death under his watch.

His prisoner chose that moment to remind Quinn of his presence. Again. "Hey lawman. I'm hungry. Mawshall said you were required to feed me. So, feed me!" The man's lament could be heard even through the closed adjoining door.

A heavy sigh escaped Quinn. He thought when he arrived in this quiet little town, he could relax and find some peace. "What happened to peace on earth, good will toward men?" Quinn grumbled under his breath. Christmas was six weeks away and he was far from achieving that Christmas spirit he had hoped for. "Shut up, Bishop. I'm goin' to see about your dinner. You belly-aching about it isn't gonna make me move any faster. Just sit back and be quiet why don't you."

Quinn jammed his hat back on his head and shoved his arms into his damp coat sleeves. Thank goodness the collar and cuffs were lined with thick beaver fur. The cold could cut a man in two if he wasn't careful out there. The walk to the Widow Lawrence's house was a short one but it was gonna be a bone-chilling night.

He pulled his revolver from the holster and rolled the cylinder of his Colt Peacemaker against his palm, listening to the clicks and watching for an empty chamber. He wondered what an odd name for an object capable of taking a life. He supposed in the right hands, this gun could be a deterrent to crime. A peacemaker—that was, *if* men valued their lives above fortune. Most of the men he dealt with bet their lives they could steal a fast buck and get away with it. The law was bettin' they couldn't.

Satisfied he was prepared for trouble, he slipped the gun back into the leather holster. He checked the short leather cord attached to base of his holster strapped to his right thigh. He vowed he was done with killin' when he left the war. So far, he had managed to keep that vow, but a lawman never knew how the day was gonna end when he pinned that tin star to his chest and strapped his guns around his hips each morning.

Quinn stepped outside into the cold and locked the door behind him. Trudging through the heavy snow, he crossed the street and walked down the boardwalk to the Widow Lawrence's house at the end of the street. He had an agreement with the widow to provide three square meals for him and any prisoners he had to hold over in his jail more than twenty-four hours.

A quick glance toward the darkened windows of his own three-room house across the street revealed its occupants had gone to bed. There was not even the faintest glow of a single oil lamp to indicate anyone lived there. From the anger his wife displayed toward him earlier, come mornin', she just might decide not to be.

Loneliness competed with the cold and Quinn turned away from the house he hoped this new bride of his would make into a home. Perhaps tomorrow's sun would bring new light to his dark and dreary world.

Quinn knocked on the widow's door. Mrs. Lawrence answered right away. "Sheriff. Please come in. I've got your prisoner's food already to go." The woman stepped back and invited him inside. The aroma of beef stew and cornbread hit him hard in his empty stomach. He closed the door to the cold, his heart as heavy as his wet coat.

CHAPTER 4

$\mathcal{I}$t was getting late, and Sarah was exhausted. The trip. The wedding. The revelation that she was now married to a Union soldier. Ex-soldier, but still—

Sarah stared out the front room's darkened window for the hundredth time. She thought about the recent turn of events once more and wondered, was she being fair to the man who had agreed to marry her and take her daughter as his own? If he hadn't, she might have lost Becca to William's parents for good and that was a prospect unthinkable.

Sarah turned away from the window once more and placed another log in the grate. Satisfied the fire wouldn't go out for quite some time, she pulled her shawl across her shoulders and sat in the only chair in the room, a solid looking rocking chair with years of wear.

Alone in the quiet of the night, Sarah finally studied her new home in detail. The cabin appeared quite small and the furnishings sparse at best—nothing at all like the lavish behemoths she lived in back in South Carolina.

She wished she could take back her words to her new husband. It wasn't his fault her life was so depressing. And she sounded selfish. She wasn't. At least, she hoped she was not stained by her in-laws condescending and arrogant ways.

Sarah took another glance around the rough-around-the-edges little house. It was warm and safe and dry. There was room enough to make a little bedroom for Becca in that tiny little storage room Quinn had referred to. All in all, she supposed things could have gone much worse for her and Becca.

Sarah's thoughts turned once more to her daughter. Becca was exhausted and fussy and confused. She just wanted to go home where everything was familiar. Sarah couldn't blame her. She felt much the same way. She did her best to calm her daughter's fears. It didn't help that the cheap coal oil lamps cast mysterious shadows on the wall and fueled her daughter's imagination.

The shadows moved and danced in the flickering lamplight. Her daughter was suspicious of them all, but Sarah was able to convince Becca to lie still long enough and listen to her favorite Christmas story. Within minutes, Becca was fast asleep, her chest rising and falling with deep, even breaths. Sarah breathed a sigh of relief.

The clock on the wall chimed the time again. It was really getting late. She wanted to apologize to Quinn, but she would have to wait until tomorrow. It wouldn't be appropriate for her to leave Becca sleeping alone and traipse down to the jail to talk to him tonight. Worried thoughts skittered across her troubled mind. What if he didn't give her the chance to apologize? What if her thoughtless accusation made him change his mind about keeping her as a bride? Could he do that here in Montana Territory? Could a man set aside his wife after only one night?

Anxiety pushed her tired, aching body to stand. Sarah walked to the front window again. The snow fell heavy. She rubbed away the frost on the window to get a better look.

Snow wasn't something that occurred much in Charleston. She couldn't remember the last time—

A familiar hat and coat appeared through the darkness and huddled against the swirling snow. Her new husband's tall form walked across the street and down the boardwalk. She kept her eyes on him. He walked past the saloon, off the boardwalk, past another house until he stopped at an open gate through a white picket fence at the end of the street.

"Where is he going?" Sarah wondered. He had said he was going to check on his prisoner. Or go to work. Or something. She had been so angry when he left, she didn't pay any attention to what he said to her.

She strained her eyes through the frosted glass panes of the front window staring down the street, doing her best to keep her new husband in sight, when he stopped and turned up the pathway to the little house's porch.

She watched him knock on the door. Immediately, someone answered the door. Sarah's heart punched at her ribs as the truth made itself known to her. She could see a brief outline of a woman's skirt at the door. The woman pulled him inside her home and closed the door behind them.

Sarah stepped away from the window, the facts were right in front of her. There was only one reason for a man to pay such a late-night visit to a woman. How dare he promise to love and honor one moment and then seek the comfort of another woman's arms the next.

Sarah's agitation pushed her back and forth across the rough wooden floor of her new home. What was she supposed to think of her husband's behavior? He had knelt down and offered a heartfelt promise to Becca. And yet, her eyes didn't deceive her. She knew what she had seen. A tryst. A tawdry affair. *Just like William.*

As much as it pained her to realize she had married her

husband's enemy, she was wise enough to also realize keeping the man as her husband was the only way to stay at arm's length from the Caldwell's money and power. He said he would love, honor and protect until they parted n death. For Becca's sake, she intended to hold him to that promise or there was gonna be hell to pay.

Funny. Thoughts of William's indiscretions didn't hurt as much as they once had, but did it really matter now? *Men.* If only she had the means or independence to choose her own destiny. She would take Becca and go someplace where no one knew her and start over. That was what she thought she did when she left Charleston. Now, she was in the same kind of marriage to the same kind of man.

Was there no man on this earth who would love her with all his heart and soul? A man who would keep himself faithful only to her? One who would protect her and her daughter from harm?

With a heartfelt sigh, she knew the answer to her questions. No, all men were created to behave the same way and all women were destined to endure. Like it or leave it had always been William's response. She wondered how this husband would respond when he learned she knew of his infidelity? Did it matter?

Sarah turned away from the dark streets and walked across the front room to the bedroom where Becca slept in peaceful slumber. No sense in wishing for something that wasn't possible. She turned down the bedroom's oil lamp flame to a tiny quiver of light. If Becca woke in the night, she would have light to see her new and unfamiliar surroundings.

Sarah undressed in the semi-darkness and slipped into the bed beside her daughter. The sheets were clean, and she snuggled closer to Becca's body for warmth. This was supposed to be her wedding night—

She was glad Quinn had left her in peace. She knew the time would come when he would demand his rights as her husband. But not tonight. No, tonight, he sought pleasures in the arms of another woman. Sarah told herself that was just fine with her, even as a lone tear slid down her cheek to say otherwise.

~

Quinn spent the entire night trying to find a comfortable position in which to sleep. His office chair was a poor excuse for a bed, that much was certain. Perhaps he should put a cot in his office for nights such as this. It made more sense than trying to sleep upright.

He stood and rubbed his cramped muscles. His six-foot two frame didn't fold up as easily as it had in his younger days. At thirty-three, his body had seen its share of abuse and he was paying the price now. A lesson to pass on to his children. *His children.*

Quinn shook the thought away and stood to put another stick of wood into the stove. The cast iron radiated heat long after the last of the flames dwindled during the night.

A nagging voice from the only occupied jail cell poked at his tiredness. "Sheriff? You up yet? I'm hungry. Mawshall said you had to—"

His irritation got the better of him. "Yeah, Johnny, I know. The marshal said I had to feed you. It's too damn early, besides you had dinner late so shut up and go back to sleep. I'll let you know when breakfast is ready."

"Damn, Sheriff. If I'da knowed you was such a cranky lawman, I woulda requested different accommodations."

"Yeah, yeah. Like you had a choice, Bishop. Now go back to sleep. The sun's not up yet."

Quinn shook his head in exasperation. He had to give

credit to his cocky prisoner for being such a charming talker. The man had a way about him that made a person forget he was a criminal. *Almost.*

Quinn set the jail's tin coffee pot on top of the flat surface of the hot stove. He had prepared the pot last night after he returned from the widow's house, getting Johnny Boy's late dinner. He was grateful to Flora for agreeing to provide his prisoner's three-square meals until the prison wagon came through town to take him away. Her delicious beef stew, hot corn bread and butter filled both his empty belly and that of his unwanted nuisance of a prisoner.

It suddenly dawned on him that if he hadn't eaten dinner until visiting Flora, then neither had his new family. He smacked himself on the forehead. What a dolt he was.

He pulled the curtain back and saw the dawn sky lighten in the east. Was it too early to head to the house? He didn't want to wake them, but if they were up wouldn't they be famished? He could kick himself. He wasn't used to thinking about someone else. That was something he would work on starting this moment.

The sound of boots on frozen snow crunched before the door to his office opened and the man he hoped to hire as his permanent deputy stepped inside.

"Whewwwwweeee, it's cold this mornin'." Eugene Phillips stood next to the stove and absorbed the heat to warm his bare hands. "Coffee ready?" He nodded to the tin coffee pot.

"Just about. Set it on the stove about five minutes ago and the fires burnin' hot so it shouldn't be long now."

Eugene nodded. "You stay here all night?" He frowned in Quinn's direction. "Don't seem right with a new bride and all." The lanky kid of about twenty raised his eyebrows in question.

Quinn knew what he was getting at and he didn't want to have this conversation. "Couldn't be helped. You still interested in a full-time job as my deputy, Eugene? Now that I have a family, I'm not gonna be able to work twenty-four hours a day, every day like I've been doing."

The coffee perked and bubbled in the pot. Eugene made himself at home and pulled two tin cups off pegs on the wall and filled them both to the brim with hot, black coffee strong enough to stand a spoon on end. He handed one to Quinn and took the chair next to the desk leaving Quinn no choice but to sit in his own chair and join him or appear unsociable. He wasn't about to offend the young man he was countin' on to help him. He needed him.

Quinn sat in his desk chair and warmed his hands on the hot tin cup. He waited for Eugene to sip his coffee and get comfortable before he asked again. "So whatta you say, Eugene? Interested in the job? The pay ain't great and there's always a chance you'll end up in the cemetery at the end of the day, but you get to know the satisfaction of keeping honest, law-abiding citizens safe from offenders like what's sitting in that cell back there—"

"I can hear ya talkin', lawman. Don't think I don't know you is castin' calumnies on my character." A voice hollered loud and clear from the cell area behind the half-opened door.

Eugene grinned and leaned closer, lowering his voice to keep the prisoner from hearing. "He sounds like a character. What's 'calumnies' mean? What'd he do anyway?"

Quinn grimaced. "Calumnies is a fancy word for lies or slander." Quinn spoke up so his prisoner could hear his words. "And no, Bishop, there's no lies goin' on here. You were charged with robbin' a bank up near Great Falls and you got caught. You sayin' that's a lie?"

No sound came from the cell. "That's what I thought. Now mind your own business." Quinn grinned at Eugene and continued his story. "The law caught him coming out of the bank. He emptied his gun into the town's deputy, then he grabbed a bystander's pistol and held a woman hostage. When the sheriff arrived, the woman got caught in the crossfire. I'm sad to say she was killed outright."

Eugene's grin slipped, and his eyes grew hard. "That ain't right. Ain't right atall usin' an innocent woman to keep his own sorry hide safe."

Quinn watched the young man cut his eyes toward the jail cell in disgust. Then he nodded in Quinn's direction. This time he raised his voice, so the prisoner could hear every word he spoke.

"Yes, sir, Sheriff Cassidy. I'll take that job as your deputy. I sure enuf will. And if I can keep some murdering thief from killing another innocent woman, why, I'd be honored." Quinn's prisoner remained quiet.

Relief must have been evident on Quinn's face because Eugene stood and stuck out his hand. "Shake on it, Sheriff Cassidy. And pin that star on me. I'm on duty startin' right now so you can go home to that new little family of yourn."

Quinn grinned and shook Eugene's hand. "Glad to have you on my side, son." Quinn pulled a worn dog-eared bible out of his top desk drawer and pushed it in Eugene's direction. "Now, lay your left hand on the bible, raise your right hand and repeat after me. I, Eugene Phillips, do hereby swear to uphold the laws as set forth by this office."

Exhaustion from spending the night in a wooden bow-back chair disappeared from Quinn's body as he administered the oath of a lawman to his new deputy. He was suddenly anxious to get home to his bride and convince her he wasn't the enemy, at least not anymore.

CHAPTER 5

*S*arah woke at dawn's first light. She sensed something had woken her, but her brain was still wrapped in a sleep induced fog. *Bacon.* Her stomach rumbled with a very unladylike growl.

"Good. You're awake. I thought you might be hungry this morning since you didn't have supper last night." The deep voice of her new husband pulled her attention to the bedroom's open door.

Quinn was standing in the doorway, his striking good looks capturing her full attention. She was awake in an instant and her breath stalled somewhere between her lungs and her throat. And her mouth went completely dry, not a smidgeon of moisture could she produce when she caught sight of Quinn's rolled up shirt sleeves exposing his muscular bare arms covered in...was that flour?

Another loud rumble from the direction of her empty stomach had her grimacing with embarrassment, but the grin stretching across Quinn's handsome face would have left her weak at the knees—had she been standing. Instead, she was in her nightgown, still lying in bed. *His* bed.

The intimacy of the moment struck her, and she needed time to guard herself against this man's charms, especially after witnessing his despicable behavior late last night.

Sarah placed a finger to her lips and pointed to Becca, but when she returned her gaze to him, he was no longer looking at her. At least not at her face. Instead, his gaze had ventured south. She looked down to see what had captured his attention. The ribbon holding the drawn neck of her nightgown had come undone in her sleep. The soft pale flesh of the rounded tops of her breasts were in full view.

Embarrassment heated her cheeks. She pulled the bedcovers to her neck, then stole a glance in his direction. He met her embarrassed gaze with a heated look that set her core to weeping. When was the last time a man had looked at her with such hunger in his eyes? *A very, very long time.*

"I think I'll give you some privacy, so you can dress. Meet me in the kitchen when you're ready," he said, his words soft and low for Becca's sake. She managed a nod before he added, "Don't take too long. Gravy's gettin' cold." He grinned.

The devastating sight of his full lips stretched over even white teeth in a charming grin pushed a shiver of something delicious across her skin. She tugged the bedcovers closer and nodded in response. He pulled the door closed behind him and she was left with a gut-punching reaction to the stranger in the next room who was now her husband. A cheating husband, she reminded herself.

A cranky groan signaled her daughter was waking. Sarah took a deep breath and prayed God would gift her with more patience to deal with her unhappy little girl and her uncensored outbursts.

She looked around the small, sparse bedroom. She mentally prepared for another day. Somehow, she had to convince her daughter they were in a better place than they had been back in Charleston. She only hoped she could convince herself of that same truth.

Fifteen minutes later, Sarah and Becca made their first appearance of the day. The smell of food permeated the little house and Sarah's stomach growled again.

She knew Quinn was in the kitchen because of the banging and rattling coming from that direction. She ushered Becca through the kitchen door in front of her. The sight that greeted her kicked her pulse from a steady trot to a full-out run. Sarah inhaled a breath to calm it down before it ran away with her completely.

Quinn stood in the kitchen with his back to her. He was shirtless. She had never seen a man in the kitchen, much less one that was half dressed. It was a treat she had no clue she had been missing.

"I'm hungry," complained Becca.

Quinn whirled at the sound of her daughter's voice. "Well, hello my sleeping beauties. I hope you're hungry. It seems I got a bit carried away with breakfast this morning."

My sleeping beauties. William had never bothered to use terms of endearment. He said it showed a man's weakness.

Sarah saw the realization dawn on Quinn's face that he was shirtless. He grabbed his shirt off the back of one of the wooden ladder-backed chairs at the kitchen table and held it up in front of him, covering his naked chest and stomach. "I'm sorry. I must be such a sight this morning."

And what a sight he was—

Sarah realized he was speaking again. She forced her eyes to his face in an attempt to distract her from his uncovered magnificence.

"Um, I broke an egg down the front of my shirt, but I didn't want to disturb you ladies to get a clean shirt, so I waited until—well, you're here now. Please. Sit down. Dig in.

I'll go grab that fresh shirt from my—our—bedroom. Be back in a minute."

Quinn held his egg covered shirt in front of him and slipped past them. His arms bulged when he clasped the soiled shirt to hide his nakedness. He disappeared from the kitchen on his way to the bedroom, but not before Sarah caught quite the view of his retreating backside. Long muscles corded his back and shoulders. She should have been ashamed of herself, gawking at the man who was still a stranger to her even though they were a wedded couple in the eyes of the law. A proper southern lady would have turned her head in modesty. And yet, her eyes followed him with a shameless curiosity she didn't know she possessed.

Just before he disappeared around the corner, she caught sight of several white raised scars on his left side that disappeared beneath the waist of his jeans. It was obvious to her now he had suffered a horrible injury. She wondered if it was from the war.

Shame punched Sarah in the gut as her cruel and thoughtless words from the previous night resurfaced. *Of course, they were from the war, you ninny.*

"Momma, I'm hungry. Can we eat now?"

Becca's whines pulled Sarah from her thoughts. "Yes, darling. See all the wonderful food Mr. Cassidy, I mean Quinn, prepared for us. Here, you sit in this chair and I'll dip your food into your plate."

Sarah helped Becca on to one of the side chairs and placed the cloth napkin from the table on her lap. She spooned food onto her daughter's plate and set the fare in front of her. Gratitude to her new husband for his kind gesture filled her troubled heart with remorse. Perhaps she had judged him too quickly.

She took a seat at the end of the table and helped herself to bacon, eggs, biscuits, butter and jelly. Mr. Cassidy, umm, the sheriff—*her husband*, returned to the kitchen fully clothed. He smiled at her and headed for the stove. "Coffee?" He held up the pot in question.

She nodded her approval. He poured the strong black beverage into her cup and joined them at the small wooden table in the tiny little kitchen. He offered her another handsome grin and gestured toward the mounds of food on the table. "I kinda got carried away cookin' this morning. I hope you have a big appetite."

There was no doubt in Sarah's mind she had an appetite alright. She realized her appetite craved something more than the mounds of food on the table could offer. And for the first time in her life, she knew what it felt like to lust after a man.

Her mother-in-law would be beside herself if she knew what was going through Sarah's mind at this moment. A satisfied grin spread across her face at the wicked thought. "Oh yes. I find I have a much bigger appetite than I ever imagined."

"It's the mountain air." Her new husband said between mouthfuls of food disappearing from his plate.

"Of course, that must be it." She followed his lead and dug in. For a few moments, no one spoke. Only the ring of metal utensils clanged on tin plates.

Soon, bellies were full and an awkward silence demanded someone to say something. Sarah did owe the man an apology for her vicious accusations. But before she could find the right words to express her regret, Quinn spoke first.

"Sarah, I know Angel Creek is a far cry from Charleston —and I'm a far cry from your first husband, but everyone suffered from that damned war. Think about it. Death and destruction did not discriminate based upon the color of a soldier's uniform. Widows and orphans are scattered from the southernmost point of this nation—and all points north.

"I did my duty just as your husband did. We each swore oaths, as soldiers, and we honored those oaths. I didn't start that war and neither did the poor men who fought and died on those battlefields. We were all victims of the carnage—you, me, Becca, your late husband. Isn't it damned time we find a way to put the past behind us and make a new start as a family?"

A glance at her husband's earnest expression convinced her she would certainly like to try.

"Momma, he said damn again." Becca pointed out between bites of food.

"Yes, dear. I heard him."

Quinn offered another apology. "I'm sorry. Like I said, I'm not used to watching my language around—"

Sarah held up her hand to stop him.

"Quinn, I would like to offer you a heartfelt apology of my own for my behavior last night. It was my exhaustion speaking and not my heart. I hope you can forgive me."

Her new husband took a deep breath and nodded, relief etched across his face. "Yesterday was exhausting for everyone. I am glad to see you won't hold my past against me." He aimed another devastating smile in her direction. She couldn't think of a single word in response. Instead, she offered him a smile of her own.

Quinn rose from his chair, pulling her improper thoughts to his handsome face. "I hate to leave you with all the dishes, but I need to check on my new deputy. Then, I'll catch a few hours of sleep over at the boardinghouse, so you and Becca won't have to tiptoe around me here. I'll be back for supper. If there's anything you need in the meantime, tell the Westons over at the mercantile to put what you need on my account."

He pushed his arms through his coat sleeves and stuffed his cowboy hat on his head. A quick nod and he was gone.

She didn't know how to scrub dishes. She didn't know how to clean a house. And she didn't know how to cook a lick. "Supper?" He was going to be back for supper. Whatever was she going to do?

She had no skills as a homemaker. She couldn't bake. She didn't even know how to fry an egg or a strip of bacon. And with a young daughter underfoot, it would be nearly impossible to keep her lack of basic skills a secret for long.

She looked around the tiny house once more. She supposed with a little work, it could be cozy. She shook her head in denial. It was going to take a lot of work and she knew nothing about that sort of thing. Nothing at all.

Despair kicked her in the chest as the full consequences of her situation met the light of morning. It was one thing to convince a stranger to marry her. It was quite another to convince him to stay married to her.

Quinn left his house and walked three doors down to his office. He hadn't realized how convenient living in town was. It did have a few drawbacks though. Angel Creek was small enough he could walk anywhere in town he wanted to go. But that meant he wasn't able to ride his horse as often as he would like. And selling ole' Jack wasn't an option. Hell would freeze over before he would even consider selling that old war horse.

He kept Jack stabled for the most part. It was expensive, but he didn't mind the cost. That blue roan gelding had saved his hide more than once during the war. He owed him a good retirement with a warm stall, all the hay and grain he could eat and an occasional gallop among the pines. It was past time he paid ole Jack a visit, but he needed to make his morning rounds first. Maybe he'd go later in the afternoon, after he got at least a few hours of sleep.

His full belly pressed against his britches. He had outdone himself with breakfast. And he had to admit, he liked cooking for his family. *Family.* That word still sounded so foreign after all this time on his own, but he hoped to convince his new wife and daughter he was in this marriage to stay and he would do everything he could to make them both feel safe and happy and cared for. He was even hopeful Sarah was warming up to him a little bit, that is, if her apology to him after breakfast was any indication.

It was a big relief after last night's rocky start, when Sarah verbally flailed him for her husband's death, to know it was her exhaustion hurling the bitter accusations at him and not her convictions.

He nodded to Ona Jenkins when he passed her bakery shop. The smell of fresh baked bread permeated the streets. Yesterday's snowfall cast an almost magical touch over Angel Creek and the crisp clear air invigorated him. Once the sun rose over the tall pines high enough to chase away the shadows, the crystalline snowflakes would shimmer and sparkle, transforming everything into a winter wonderland. It was a perfect setting for a holiday miracle and he vowed to do his very best to make this a Christmas to remember for Sarah's daughter. *His daughter.*

Quinn nodded to several early passersby during his morning rounds about town. He circled back down the last street and headed to his office. Stomping his boot heels against each other, he removed as much snow as possible and stepped inside his office.

"Good mornin', Eugene. Any problems with the prisoner?" Quinn headed for the coffee pot. He was grateful his deputy liked his coffee strong too.

"Nah, prisoner's been sleeping sound. That is, 'till about

five minutes ago. He's bellyaching again for food. I hope the man ain't gonna be here long. His appetite'll break your sheriffin' budget."

"The US marshal that dropped him off said a prison wagon should be through here sometime in the next day or so, but with this snow and the melt, it might be tough getting that heavy prison wagon through the mud. I'm afraid he might be with us a while."

Eugene nodded and pulled his coat and hat from the rack by the front door. "Why you back so soon? I thought you was gonna spend time with that new family of yourn, maybe take in some shut eye seein' as how you was up all night and all."

"I wanted to let you get some sleep as soon as I could. I'll catch a few hours of shut-eye this afternoon when I finish my rounds. Tonight will be your first all night shift. You need to be on your toes in case ole' Johnny back there has some friends who'd like to pay him a visit."

"You think he's got some friends that'll traipse through snow to bust him out?" Eugene frowned at the possibility.

"Hard to say. Depends on whether Mr. Bishop's got some resources. Money is always a motivator for a man who has larceny in his blood."

Eugene nodded in agreement. "I'll get goin' then, Sheriff. Be back about four." The tall, lanky kid turned to leave when Quinn called out to him.

"Hey, Eugene? How about you call me Quinn."

His new deputy grinned in response. "Be proud to, Quinn. Be mighty proud to."

Eugene left to grab some shut-eye. Quinn sat down in his chair and rubbed his gritty eyelids. He needed some sleep too. He had been up over twenty-four hours and in that time span, he had acquired a new family, a new prisoner, and a new deputy. Life was funny sometimes. A man never knew what to expect when he got up in the morning.

A small knock on his office door announced a visitor. He looked at the clock on the wall. *Ten o'clock.* Most folks in town didn't knock. They just walked right on in.

He checked his side arm just in case this wasn't a friendly visit. Quinn strode to the door prepared for anything, but he wasn't prepared for this.

"Sarah? What are you doing here? Where's Becca?" Quinn stepped back and let his new wife enter his domain. He closed the door behind her and offered her the chair Eugene had just vacated moments ago.

"Charity came over this morning for a visit and I asked her to keep an eye on Becca for a few moments—so I could come here." Sarah took the chair he offered.

She had a nervousness about her that made Quinn uneasy. "Is everything alright?" He hoped he hadn't done anything wrong at breakfast.

"Yes, yes. Everything is fine." She hesitated and then her shoulders slumped. "No, everything isn't fine. There's— something I need to discuss with you. Something that should have been settled sooner, I suppose."

Quinn's heart dropped to his stomach. He thought after she apologized, any differences they may have had were behind them. But something troubled his bride from Charleston. What on earth could have gone wrong between breakfast and now?

He could see her hands tremble. He didn't want to ever cause her any despair. "Whatever it is, Sarah, you can tell me. Just say it."

She nodded and bowed her head for a moment. Then, she squared her shoulders and stiffened her spine. Whatever was bothering her was difficult to share but he could see her determination and he admired her courage.

"I need to tell you—" She hesitated again, and it seemed her courage faltered.

"Go on, Sarah. Tell me what it is that has you so troubled."
Quinn kneeled in front of her and took her shaking hands
into his own. He smiled his encouragement and hoped she
knew he was not someone to fear.

"I—" she hesitated and then her words rushed out in rapid
succession. "I need some money for Becca's bedroom. She
needs a place of her own."

Relief flooded Quinn's body. "Is that what this is about?
Gosh, Sarah. You had me 'bout scared outta my wits."

Tears glistened in her eyes and a single crystal drop slid
down her cheek. She swiped it away with one gloved hand.

"Ah, Sarah. Don't cry. I didn't forget. I told you I'd go to
the bank and let the banker know you could have access to
all of my money. I just haven't had time to do it this morning,
but I'll do it first chance I get. I promise. You and Becca will
have everything you need.

"I'm not a wealthy man, but I have some money from my
family's estate, and I've got my salary here and my military
pension." He pulled her into his arms and held her trembling
body tight against his.

Quinn wanted to comfort Sarah, but an unexpected bolt
of desire shot through his body and straight to his southern
region. The feel of her body touching his made him want
more—much more—but his desires would have to wait. She
was still coming to grips with being married to a stranger.
He would not rush her into his bed. He wanted her to come
of her own accord, however long that took.

He stepped back and pulled her face up with his finger.
"Look at me, Sarah. Anything you need, anything at all, all
you have to do is ask. Understand?"

Her face was flushed with emotion. She nodded her
understanding and wiped at her face.

"Now, you go down to Mr. Weston's mercantile and you
tell Jeremiah or his wife, Cassie, to put anything you need on

my account. Becca needs her own room and you have my permission to make it happen."

Sarah hesitated and Quinn wondered if there was more. Then she nodded. Relief deflated his lungs and he grinned at her, hoping to ease all her fears. When she smiled back at him, it was the most beautiful sight he had ever seen.

"Now, you go on. By supper tonight, I want Becca to have the most beautiful bedroom a little girl could ever want."

A grimace appeared on Sarah's face. "Speaking of supper, the Reverend Tilly and his wife invited us for dinner tonight."

Quinn fought back a groan. He was dog tired and he wanted nothing more than to eat supper with his wife and daughter, then fall into bed and sleep until morning. But, if Sarah wanted to eat at the reverend's house, he wouldn't disappoint her.

CHAPTER 6

*S*arah allowed Quinn to walk her to the door. Once outside, she headed in the direction of the mercantile since Quinn watched her walk down the street.

She'd had every intention of telling him she had no domestic skills when she went to his office that morning. And yet, when she'd gotten there, she just couldn't get the words to come out of her mouth. Instead, she said the first thing that came to mind: *Becca needed a room of her own.* She hadn't thought herself such a coward.

Quinn had surprised her with his generosity. It was overwhelming to think he trusted her completely. Her guilt mocked her when she stepped inside the mercantile. *You are a fraud, Sarah Caldwell Cassidy. A complete and total fraud. Quinn deserves better.*

"Can I help you, ma'am?" the gentleman behind the counter asked.

Sarah knew she had a lot of things to sort out, but Becca did need her own room. She would try to find another opportunity to tell Quinn that she had no idea how to cook.

Or clean. Or sew. Or—later. Right now, she owed it to Quinn to at least act like a suitable wife.

"I need some things for my new home. The sheriff— Sheriff Cassidy, I mean Quinn—my husband—"

"Oh yes, good morning Mrs. Cassidy. I heard about the wedding yesterday. Congratulations to you and Quinn. I hope you two will be as happy as me and my missus have been all these years. Now, what can I do fer ya." The kindly man picked up his pen and paper ready to take down her order. She was certain he could see right through her guise but his friendly demeanor seemed genuine.

"Um, well—my daughter, Rebecca—I have a daughter and she's six and she needs a room of her own. The sheriff's house isn't big enough and—"

"Say no more, Mrs. Cassidy," the man interrupted her with a friendly wave of his hand. "Mrs. Weston has a lot of experience with little girl's bedrooms. We have five girls of our own. Cassie, can you come out here please? This lady needs your assistance."

The man's wife came out from behind the curtain separating the store front from the back. "Well, hello. You must be new in town. I haven't seen you around."

"Yes, I arrived by stage coach yesterday. I was married to the sheriff, Quinn Cassidy."

"Oh, you are one of the mail order brides I been hearing about. Can't say as you look any different than any other bride in town. You say you married the sheriff, did ya?"

"Yes, I did. Yesterday." Finishing school hadn't prepared Sarah for how to handle a conversation of this nature. Did she try to explain her circumstances? No, that would only invite trouble if someone found out she could be a wanted fugitive. How could she explain why she was forced to steal her own daughter from her in-laws'? How would Quinn deal with the news? Her stomach roiled at the thought.

"Well, welcome to our little town," Mrs. Weston said. "You caught yourself a right fine man there in Quinn Cassidy. There'll be some broken-hearted ladies about town when word gets out you snatched him up right from under their noses."

Sarah didn't know what to say so she smiled and nodded in agreement. She supposed she was lucky that a man like Quinn had chosen her considering—

"Now, tell me what I can help you with this mornin'," Mrs. Weston said, leaving Sarah no time for second-guessing.

Sarah didn't have a clue where to start. She had always had someone in charge of everything. Would Mrs. Weston guess she was a fraud?

"We just moved into the sheriff's house and we need—"

"Say no more. I'll bet you're here to order things to fix up that little house the sheriff is renting. I don't blame ya. A woman can't make a cozy home for a man with sticks and stones. Now, let's check the stock room and see what I have for immediate use. Then, we'll order everything else."

Relief flooded Sarah's nerves and soothed them enough to relax. Mrs. Weston took charge and before she knew it, the stack of items growing in the middle of the mercantile's wooden countertop was over Mr. Weston's head. But when her new friend slammed the catalog of supplies closed, Sarah's stomach plummeted.

"That is an awful lot of stuff. Maybe we should put some of it back, I mean, I don't think my husband had any idea how much money this was going to cost—"

"I had a notion or two." Sarah spun toward the familiar voice, goosepimples dotting her skin underneath her warm clothing.

"Quinn. What are you doing here?" Sarah's voice sounded breathy to her own ears. The grin on her husband's face indicated he heard it too.

"I was headed to the boardinghouse for some shut eye for a few hours while Willie over at the stables keeps an eye on my prisoner. I was on my noon rounds around town when I saw you through the window. Looks like a lot of things there." Quinn pointed to the pile of items on the counter.

"I, I know. I was just telling Mrs. Weston I think we overdid it and I'm trying to decide what to put back."

Quinn stood in front of her and pulled her close, his hands firm and warm on her shoulders. He looked down at her, his hazel eyes dotted with specs of gold captured hers and she lost all ability to think or breathe or speak.

"Sarah." His breath fanned her face. Ripples of heat tumbled one over another over another until they all landed in a pile at a certain place she was suddenly very much aware of. "I said I would provide whatever you need to buy to make that old house into a home for us. I meant it. You have my permission to buy anything you need. Do you understand what I'm saying?"

His look of earnest appeal pricked her doubting heart. Did she understand what he meant? Was he saying he wanted her to make them a home and he would abandon his philandering ways and honor his wedding vows to her? Did she dare to dream this marriage could become a real marriage? Her pulse hiccupped in anticipation.

Quinn leaned in and kissed her temple. The intimacy of his kiss warmed her cheeks, but it was his earthy smell of pine and horse and cold outdoors that made her stomach flip flop, once again leaving her breathless.

He squeezed her shoulders before he let her go. He nodded to the mercantile owners watching everything from behind the counter and he restated his intentions. "Mrs. Weston, would you please help Sarah with anything she needs and put it on my account. I'll be by at the end of the week to settle up. Now, I'm gonna catch a few hours of sleep and get back on duty until Eugene comes in late this afternoon."

Quinn tipped his hat to her and gifted her with another beautiful smile before he disappeared out into the bright sunlit day. Sarah stood frozen in place long after he had left the store. She mentally scrutinized his good looks and willed herself to capture his masculine scent. William had smelled of toilet water and tobacco. She had always thought the scents made him seem more masculine somehow—that is, until now.

"Well now, Mrs. Cassidy. I'd say we just received your husband's approval to make that little house into Angel Creek's newest showcase. Let's wrap these things up, shall we? I'll send them over to your home so you can get started on that redecorating."

Sarah pulled her thoughts away from Quinn and back to her purchases piled high on the counter. Cassie Weston sidled up to her and said in a conspiratorial whisper. "I think your new husband is quite smitten with you, Mrs. Cassidy. And, I think ordering a mail order bride was just what the sheriff needed. Now, let's get this stuff boxed up and I'll have my stock boy cart them over to you later this morning."

Sarah nodded absentmindedly to the woman's chatter while gazing at the door where Quinn disappeared. Was her husband smitten with her? A delicious sensation coursed through her body. She hoped so. At least, she hoped he was smitten enough to be willing to leave his philandering ways behind—and overlook the fact she had no domestic skills. And ignore the possibility of an arrest warrant landing on his desk with her name on it. Dear Lord, she really did need a Christmas miracle—or two.

Quinn sat at his desk in his office and sipped on his third cup of coffee. He'd had a hard time waking up after only three hours of sleep, and the early winter darkness hadn't helped spark his vitality. A quick glance at the clock on the wall indicated Eugene would be arriving soon to start his shift.

He stood and walked to the window peering out into the fading daylight. Soon, the winter darkness would be complete and the few gas lights standing on each side of the street would illuminate the frozen crystals in the snow. He hoped the snow would remain until Christmas.

Pine tree branches hung low with the weight of the frozen precipitation and the normally muddy streets were now sparkling white and the perfect backdrop for the perfect Christmas for his new family. *Perfect.* In a few weeks, he would bundle his family up in blankets and take them for a sleigh ride out into the forest to cut down their family's first Christmas tree.

Quinn remembered the holidays of his youth surrounded by family and friends. There was plenty of eggnog, wassail, fruit cake, and red velvet ribbons tied everywhere—on lamp posts, on wreaths hanging from front doors, on the harnesses of the draft horses adorned with brass bells.

Christmas with his family had branded such fun and warm memories on his heart, he wanted to recreate some of those wonderful memories for Becca. He wanted them to drown out the sad memories of all that little girl had lost because of the war.

He heard Eugene stomp his boots on the snow-cleared boardwalk just outside. He was glad to know his new deputy had a sense of being on time.

He opened the door but instead of his deputy, Sarah and Becca stood poised to knock.

"Sarah? What are you doing here?" he blurted before he thought how his question would sound. Quinn stepped back and ushered the ladies inside.

Sarah looked embarrassed and stammered in her response. "I—I must have misunderstood. I thought you said you would accompany Becca and I to the Reverend and Mrs. Tilly's house. For dinner."

"Yes, I did, but I planned to pick you up in the carriage, so you and Becca wouldn't have wet feet. I'm sorry. I should have been clearer about my plans."

Relief relaxed Sarah's face. "No, I should have asked."

Sarah's embarrassment settled into the pink spots on her cheeks.

"Well, no matter. You're here now. As soon as Eugene arrives, you and Becca can wait here, and I'll go hitch up the carriage. It isn't far to the reverend's home, but when the sun goes down, the temperatures plummet. It's too cold for either one of you to wade through the snow."

"Who are you?" Quinn heard Becca's question, but when he turned to see who she was speaking to, she was nowhere to be seen.

"Becca?" Sarah's puzzled expression turned to Quinn "Where is she?"

Quinn's heart punched against his ribs. He knew exactly where she was and, although she wasn't in danger, he didn't want her around a man like Bishop.

He pushed the half-opened door between his office and the prisoner's cells to see Becca next to the cell of Johnny Bishop, carrying on a conversation like they were old friends.

"Becca, come away from there," he called to the little girl.

She stomped her little foot and crossed her arms in defiance. It was a gesture he was quickly becoming very familiar with. "I don't want to. Johnny's my friend. He said so. "

Quinn moved to remove her from the cell area and away from the prisoner, when Sarah intervened.

"Becca. Do as Quinn says. Come away from there right this minute." She pushed past him and grabbed Becca's hand to pull her daughter away from the man's cell when his prisoner spoke up.

"Well, how nice to meet you too, ma'am. Why, does this cute little southern charmer belong to you? Yes, I can see she does. She's a beauty just like her momma."

Quinn could see Sarah was caught off guard by the man's manners and his southern accent. She held Becca's hand in hers, but she no longer seemed interested in making a hasty retreat.

Johnny Bishop saw it too and he made the most of his opportunity. "Now, watt's a couple a beauties like you doin' in this littl' backwoods town? You look like you should be gracin' the pawla of one of those fine mansions down south somewhera. Where you from, darlin'?"

Quinn watched Sarah hesitate, then answer the prisoner's question. "We are from Charleston. Where is your accent from, sir? I can't place it exactly."

Johnny Bishop flashed his toothy smile and leaned against the cell bars just a few feet away from Quinn's new family.

"Johnny, go sit back down. Sarah, Becca. You shouldn't be in here—" Quinn started.

"Ah, come now, Sheriff. How can I do anybody harm penned up behind these iron bars?" His prisoner shot him a knowing look before he turned his full attention back to Sarah. "And to answer your question ma'am, I'm from Nawlins. Most people not from there refer to it as New Orleans. Have you ever visited my fair city?"

Quinn saw the look of surprise on Sarah's face followed by a smile.

"I have, sir. My husband took me there once not long after we married."

"Why Sheriff, I didn't know you was the romantic type." Johnny was not making this easy on him.

"Oh, no sir. Quinn is my second husband. I am a widow—was a widow."

"From Charleston, you say? So, your husband fought for the Confederates?" Johnny asked.

"Yes, sir. He was killed this past April, just as the war was ending."

"Please accept my condolences, ma'am. I certainly feel your loss. I lost a lot of friends to those damned Yankees myself." He saw his wife's shoulders bunch at the uncomfortable turn of conversation.

Quinn decided enough was enough. "I think we should let our prisoner get some rest. Why don't we wait for Eugene in my office? He'll be along any moment."

He didn't give Sarah a chance to think about her choice. Quinn reached for Sarah's elbow and guided her out of the cell area and back into his office. He tried not to notice that she was watching the prisoner over her shoulder. Thank goodness, Sarah guided Becca along with them. The last thing he wanted was for Becca to fall victim to the charms of a criminal like Bishop.

He heard Eugene's footfalls before his deputy entered the room. Quinn watched him eye the room's occupants. He nodded to Sarah, taking his hat off and holding it in both hands. A sign of respect to a lady. Another thing Quinn liked about his new employee.

"Hey, there Sheriff. Ma'am." His deputy nodded to Becca. "Hey there little lady. Now ain't you a perty thang."

Eugene bent down on one knee, so he was almost eye to eye with Becca. The little girl was only six years old, but she already had flirting down to an art. Becca's dimples pocked her cheeks as she gave Eugene the cutest little curtsy Quinn had ever seen.

"Do you have any candy in your pocket?" Becca unabashedly asked.

"Becca, that is impolite." Sarah pulled Becca against her, holding her in place by her shoulders. "My daughter still has some things to learn—um, I'm sorry. I didn't catch your name."

Quinn stepped up and did the introductions. "Sarah, this is my new deputy, Eugene Phillips. Eugene, this is my new bride Sarah, and her daughter—our daughter—Rebecca."

If Quinn had thought about the possible repercussions of his introductions of Sarah and Becca to his deputy, he would have approached the situation differently. It never occurred to Quinn to refrain from calling Sarah's daughter their daughter. It never occurred to him to hold back his enthusiasm at being her father. And, it never occurred to him that anything would be amiss at his declaration—until the little girl ran screaming from his office and out into the cold, dark night.

"I hate you! You're not my daddy, my daddy is dead! My mommy killed him!"

CHAPTER 7

"Becca! Come back!" Sarah raced into the frigid twilight after her daughter. She knew Quinn was right behind her, but she was too worried about Becca to even think about what she was going to say to him when he had the time to question her about her daughter's accusation. *My mommy killed my daddy!*

Sarah followed Becca's little footprints in the snow. Soon, it was clear where she was headed. To the only place she knew was safe and warm and dry. The only place her little girl could call home. Their new home—Quinn's house.

Sarah slowed her walk to give Becca time to cry. She knew her daughter well enough to know exactly what she would do. What she always did when she was upset.

Becca would fling herself onto her bed and cry until she had spent all her emotions through red and puffy eyes. Then, she would snuggle next to her dog and hiccup in her exhausted sleep.

Sarah wished she had been able to bring Becca's little dog. Annabelle might have helped ease some of Becca's anxieties, but Sarah had stolen her daughter away in the middle of the night and the dog sometimes slept in Mrs. Handy's room. She hadn't been willing to take the risk of being discovered and lose her daughter for good.

Sarah reached the front door just in time to hear Becca slam it against its sturdy frame. A moment later, the sound of the bedroom door slammed inside the house. She stopped to give Becca her space. Quinn stopped behind her, his breath puffing into the cold air like little white clouds.

"Sarah, I'm so sorry. I had no idea she would be so upset. I didn't think." Quinn stood behind her on the boardwalk in front of the house, offering his apologies.

"It's not your fault, Quinn. It's just that, she's been through so much this year. And, she's only six years old. She doesn't understand about war and death. She just knows her daddy left, and he never came back. She feels like it was all her fault somehow. That is, until my in-laws told Becca that I killed her father."

"That explains her words about you killing her father. That much makes sense, but why would her grandparent's say such a thing to a little girl?"

"Because they are evil people." It was all she could say before her emotions bubbled over. Sarah couldn't stop her emotions from bubbling over so she tried to hide them behind her gloved hands. Becca wasn't the only one who needed to cry. Sarah had done her best to be strong for her daughter—the trip on the steamboat to Angel Creek hadn't been an easy one on either of them. And now her friends were scattered about with Julia and Anna living on ranches outside of town and Ruby gone with her husband some-where. It was just too much—

Strong hands squeezed her shoulders. "Sarah, what can I do to fix this?" She knew she should pull away from Quinn. She shouldn't want the feel of his arms around her. He was a stranger, and their marriage was still so new. She felt—

disloyal to William, and yet—she yearned for the strength and comfort Quinn offered.

William was dead and buried. And, he had broken their marriage vows so many times. What kind of loyalty did she owe the man who rode off to war knowing full well he had left their fate in the hands of the same parents he often spoke about with disdain.

Her loyalty now belonged to Becca and herself and what was in their best interests. She hadn't known Quinn but a little over twenty-four hours, and she yet she sensed he was the kind of man she could trust to take care of her and her little girl.

She turned and flung herself against Quinn's chest, tucking her chin into the warmth of his body. He folded her inside his warm, strong arms and remained silent, sharing his strength through his touch.

Sarah didn't know how long they stood in the quiet darkness of that early December night, but it was enough to give her thoughts a chance to explore the possibility of a future with this generous man.

She buried her face deeper into the opening of his unbuttoned coat. He must have grabbed it when he rushed after them and hadn't taken the time to fasten it closed.

The aroma of pine and leather drifted into her nose and tickled her senses. A shiver of something delicious rippled across her skin and tempted her to reach out and kiss the delicate hollow of his throat exposed by his open coat. Should she? Could she be so bold?

"Ah, Sarah. You're shivering. Let's get you inside and then we can talk about what to do."

Sarah thought about telling Quinn her shiver had nothing to do with the cold and everything to do with him. But that didn't seem an appropriate response from a mother who just witnessed her little girl run off sobbing into the night.

So instead, she said, "I think that might be the best idea, for now."

Quinn opened the door for her and ushered her inside. The room was filled with stacks and rows of goods she had purchased earlier. A sharp stab of guilt poked her in the stomach when she saw Quinn's shocked face.

"I'm sorry. I overdid it, didn't I? It's too much money. Mrs. Weston assured me I needed every single item, or I wouldn't have bought all of this...." her voice trailed off and she spread her arms to encompass the room filled to the brim with stuff.

"No, of course not. I told you to buy whatever you needed, I guess I just didn't realize how much stuff it takes to see to a woman's needs."

His words made Sarah feel even worse. "You must think me a vain and selfish person. I was planning to put a lot of this back, but Mrs. Weston insisted—"

"Nonsense, Sarah. I think nothing of the kind. I think you are used to the finer things in life, and as I'm certain you have observed, Angel Creek isn't exactly Charleston. But as I said before, I have money put back and I have my salary as a lawman and my pension from the Army, so don't fret over anything. I promise I'll see to it you and Becca have everything you need."

Sarah's emotions were still riding at the surface of her reserve. She was having a difficult time keeping her tears in check. This man was a kind and generous person. He deserved a good wife. A competent wife. He deserved a better wife than she.

Perhaps it was a good time to tell him he drew the short straw when he picked her from the mail order bride catalog or whatever he used to order himself a wife. She couldn't cook. She didn't know how to clean. She didn't know how to manage and run a household unless there were unlimited funds and a housekeeper and cook nearby. She stole a look at

Quinn's handsome face. As much as she wanted to keep him, she felt she owed it to him to tell him the truth.

"Quinn, I think maybe we should talk."

"Sure. Give me a minute. I want to check on Becca. Make sure she's doin' alright."

Before she could stop him, Quinn let himself into the little house's only bedroom and disappeared inside. She followed him to the door, determined to be close in case Becca let loose on him again.

The lone oil lamp illuminated the small room. She saw Becca laying on her side in the bed, hugging her stuffed toy. Quinn knelt beside her and propped his elbows on the bed, his head rested in his hands much like Becca did when she said her evening prayers.

Becca lay sniffing in the semi-darkness, the light from the lantern reflecting off her tear-stained cheeks. Sarah's heart ached to see her daughter's pain. If there was only something she could do.

"Becca. I'm so sorry. It was thoughtless of me to say those things. Will you let me try to explain?"

"No!" Becca's angry voice snipped at Quinn's patient one.

"Please, Becca. It's important. I want to explain. I want to fix things between us. Will you give me a chance to tell you the whole story?" Quinn peered down into Becca's face. Sarah could tell her daughter didn't want to listen, but Becca was always the curious one.

Quinn reached out to stroke the dirty fuzz from Becca's stuffed toy. Becca let him for a moment and then jerked it out of Quinn's reach. Just when Sarah thought her daughter was done listening, she sat up, crossed her legs on the bed, and hugged her toy.

Sarah held her breath. Becca leaned toward Quinn. What was she going to do? Would Becca's anger goad her into physically striking out at Quinn? Before she could warn him,

Becca leaned even closer. "Okay, you can tell me a story. And don't leave out any of the good parts either."

~

Quinn hadn't expected Becca to listen to him. She was still so angry and hurt, so when she agreed to let him tell her the whole story, his heart kicked into a full gallop.

He had intended to tell her he was sorry if she thought he was trying to take her father's place. He wanted to explain how excited he was she was now his little girl, but her misinterpretation of his words showed she was still a little girl who just wanted to be loved by her father. And Quinn wanted to be that father.

"Would it be alright if I sat next to you on the bed? Your momma can join us if she wishes."

Becca's joy at the prospect of sharing a story with her mother punched him in the gut. What must this little girl have gone through these last six months or so?

Quinn rose from his bent position on the floor and waited for Becca to slide on over to make room for him. Then, he nodded to Sarah who still watched from the door. She entered the room and walked to the far side of the bed. He felt the mattress dip when Sarah slipped into bed and lay on Becca's other side.

It was strange to be lying here in the semi-darkness of his once lonely bedroom on a cold winter's night, surrounded by females. A pleasant kind of strange though. A strange he could get used to.

"Momma, Quinn promised me a story. Where's my story?" Becca squirmed between them and he guessed he better get on with it or this situation was gonna take another turn.

"I'm gonna tell you a story. It's one of my favorites. Now,

settle back and listen real close." He turned his head and cast an amused look in Sarah's direction. She grinned at him. It was a punch-in-the-chest sight that made him hold his breath.

Sarah nodded. She must have thought his hesitation was because he was nervous. And a lesser man might be frightened of the little bundle of explosive contradictions lying between them. But Quinn wasn't afraid, although there were times she did deserve a little more barbed wire around her boundaries.

No, Quinn was afraid of this little girl's mother—his new bride. This beauty from Charleston, with the charming southern accent and quiet manners, who had only arrived yesterday and who had already stolen his heart. But how did she feel about him? He wished he knew.

"Quinn?" The excitement in Becca's voice had slipped a notch or two. He knew he better get his story started or he was gonna lose his audience.

"How about a Christmas story?" he stalled.

"Which one?" Becca wanted to know.

"Do you have a favorite one?" Quinn hadn't exactly kept up with Christmas stories. There hadn't been a need among his fellow soldiers, although he probably could have boosted morale around Christmas time had he done so.

"I like the one where Santa comes to visit with his reindeer." Becca's glee at the prospect of a magical man dropping toys and candy off at her house while she slept was adorable.

"You mean *A Visit from St. Nicholas?* I know the author," Quinn pronounced proudly.

"You do not," Sarah blurted and then caught herself, mouthing *sorry* and urging him to continue. He was happy to say his statement was one hundred percent factual.

"But I do, thank you very much, dear wife. His name is Mr. Moore, Clement C. Moore, and he is a professor of ancient language at several well-known universities. He and his family lived in the estate two properties down the Hudson River from my parents in upstate New York. He wrote the poem to amuse his half dozen children. Later, he published it in a book of his own poems. There was quite an uproar about it at the time."

"Why?" Becca's rapt attention let him know she was hooked. He cut a glance to Sarah who seemed as interested in the story as her daughter. He was delighted to have their undivided attention if only for the moment. It made him feel needed. Necessary.

"Well, Mr. Moore made up the story, and people thought he was changing Christmas traditions."

"How?" Becca's curiosity was intense.

Quinn cut an amused look over Becca's head to Sarah. The woman stole his breath away. Refocusing on Becca's question, he answered his new daughter's question.

"He wrote that Santa's reindeer knew how to fly, and he gave them each their own name. And Santa would sneak down your chimney and leave presents and candy—"

"I don't like you!" Becca suddenly screamed. She kicked out at Quinn, catching him mid-thigh with her booted heel. "Go away! You're mean. I hate you!"

Quinn's shock was paralyzing. He watched in disbelief as Sarah pulled Becca to her and held her in place. He didn't know if it was to protect her daughter or him. Either way, it was clear he wasn't wanted here anymore.

He backed out of the bedroom and closed the door behind him. *What just happened in there?*

Quinn listened at the door until Becca's angry cries had returned to quiet hiccups. Should he leave? Should he stay? He raked his fingers through his hair in exasperation. Maybe he wasn't cut out to be a father. Maybe he wasn't cut out to be a husband.

The door knob clicked behind him. He turned to see Sarah slip quietly out of the bedroom, closing the door softly behind her.

"Is she asleep?" Quinn asked.

"Yes, she's finally asleep." Sarah offered nothing more to explain the little girl's sudden mood change.

He paced the rough wooden floor, his boots scrapping across the bare surface. In frustration he raked his fingers through his hair once more. "Sarah, I don't understand what just happened—"

She pulled his hand from his head and held on to his forearm to focus his attention on her. "Quinn. She's a child. She thinks like a child. And, she certainly has inherited her father's lack of restraint. It isn't you. Really, it isn't."

Quinn pulled Sarah closer, peering down into her eyes. He wanted to know everything about Sarah and Becca's past life. But at that moment, he wanted to know what he had done wrong.

"It feels like it's me. She didn't say 'I hate the wall' or 'I hate this town.' She said, 'I hate you.' What did I do wrong this time, Sarah?" he begged for this woman to enlighten him as to how he could be a better father to Becca.

"It was the fact you said the author of the story made it all up," Sarah explained. "The flying reindeer. Santa bringing toys and candy down the chimney. Becca needs to believe that all that stuff is real. Just like she needs to believe in the possibility of a happily-ever-after. After all the heartache and loss she's had to deal with at such a young age, can't you understand how much she needs something to hang her Christmas star upon?"

Quinn felt like an idiot. Just like when he introduced her as his daughter, Becca wanted to believe her father was still alive somewhere. And just like Christmas, Becca wanted—

needed—to believe in happiness and wonder and magic and the miracles of Christmas.

"Sarah, I'm so sorry. I am so new to this family thing. I don't know how to be a father. I keep tripping over Becca's feelings. Unintentionally, but the results are just as painful all the same. I left you alone on our wedding night. I brought you to this rundown house expecting you to fix it all. I'm a sorry excuse for a man—"

"Don't say that, Quinn. It's not true. You are a wonderful, caring, generous—" Sarah seemed as much at a loss for words to describe him as he was and that didn't make him feel any better.

But, when Sarah turned her face up to his, she leaned in and kissed him—really kissed him. He had to admit, he felt a whole lot better about, well, everything.

CHAPTER 8

*S*arah had no idea what made her lean in and kiss her new husband. Maybe it was the way he cared about Becca and wanted to spare her feelings any way he could. Or, maybe it was his generosity and willingness to father that same little girl despite her prickly personality that touched Sarah's heart.

But most likely it was her attraction to the man. Could it be as simple as that? She wasn't a forward woman. Her mother hadn't raised her to be one. Perhaps that was her downfall where her first husband was concerned and it was time to try a new tactic.

Sarah leaned into Quinn and knew her actions caught him off-guard at first. Maybe he was even shocked at her forward behavior. But, she knew the moment he decided to join in. His hands pulled her closer, and he held her so tight against him, she could feel the hard muscles in his chest and stomach bunch and relax in rhythm to the movement of his roaming hands.

Sarah's skin pimpled under her clothing each time his hands circled the small of her back, or cupped the back of her head, forcing her lips to angle under his for a closer, more intimate contact. She had never been kissed—well, she had been kissed before. Of course, William had kissed her many times during their eight years of marriage. But she had never been kissed like *this* before.

She needed air. Her breath was lost somewhere between her mouth and his, and she needed air.

Sarah pulled away. At least she thought she did. But the truth was, barely the width of a hair separated her swollen, thoroughly kissed lips from Quinn's. She was no longer touching them, but the sensual feel of his warm breath caressing her face made her weak at the knees.

She lifted her eyes as far as his chin. It was such a wonderful chin too. The shadow of dark whiskers covered his small cleft indention. She remembered he hadn't taken the time to shave that morning. Under normal circumstances, she preferred a man without facial hair, but now, she wasn't so certain.

She felt his heart's rhythm beating in his chest against hers through the fabric of her dress. Her gaze wandered upward another notch to rest on his full lips. The same ones that had just kissed hers with an undeniable passion that curled her toes in delight.

He cleared his throat. The vibration in his chest pulled at her most intimate places. Sarah wanted to look straight into his eyes, but he was a head taller than her, so she tilted her chin a little higher and leaned her head back to meet his gaze.

Fringed by thick dark lashes, the warm golden color of Quinn's eyes hinted at the heat she saw in their depths. Another wave of goosebumps started at the base of her neck where his strong warm fingers held her and moved down her body to the apex of her core.

"Sarah," he breathed her name on his warm breath.

84

"I know," she whispered back. The cozy fire crackled in the grate, throwing flickering shadows on the bare floor and walls.

"I wasn't expecting...this." Quinn's gaze dropped to her mouth and heated her more than any flame of fire could. He leaned down and touched her waiting lips with a gentle kiss, so sweetly that tears stung behind her closed lids. She waited for him to deepen the kiss. And she was not disappointed.

His lips pressed into hers, the pressure increasing until her lips opened, and his hot tongue delved into her mouth, exploring until her knees nearly buckled. His hands drifted from her neck down her waist where he pulled her body tighter against his.

Her own hands created a path beneath his coat and roamed freely over his warm hard muscles hidden underneath his wool shirt. Sarah followed each line and curve with her fingers memorizing them. There were so many secrets to be discovered beneath the rough fabric.

Quinn answered her touch and pulled her closer against his body.

The sudden awareness of a new hardness south of his gun belt begged for further exploration. She wanted to claim this virile cowboy as her own, but should she? Didn't she owe him a bit more honesty about what he had gotten himself into by taking a wife such as herself?

"Sarah," Quinn whispered against her hair and wrapped his arms around her completely. Warm. Wanted. Wedded. She told herself it was perfectly acceptable to feel these feelings. In the eyes of God and the law, she could succumb to Quinn's many charms and no one would think a thing in the world about it. And yet—

"Quinn, I would like to—"

Quinn's deep voice chuckled, she felt the vibrations in his chest against her cheek when he spoke. "I would like to too.

I'd like to lay you down right here in front of the fire and show you how much I... how much we...."

Sarah was aware he couldn't bring himself to say what was in his heart. Perhaps the mercantile owner's wife was right. Maybe her new husband was smitten with her.

Perhaps it was best they left certain things unsaid. It was too soon to declare any affection for each other. They had only known each other one day. And her own heart strings were a tangled mess of doubt and confusion, for it was too soon to have any real feelings for this man. Wasn't it?

And then there was the lie. Her lie. She didn't know the first thing about making a home out of this rustic house. How on earth could she convince Quinn to let her and Becca stay when he found out she couldn't cook. She couldn't clean. And she might have an arrest warrant in her future.

And what about the possibility of William's parents showing up one day and ripping this family apart? Shouldn't Quinn know about that secret too? As much as her conscience demanded she tell him the truth, her heart resisted. She was afraid their marriage was too fragile to withstand the enormity of such a revelation.

And then there was his infidelity. What was she to do about that little fact? What could she do? If she demanded he stop, would he? Or would he do as William had done and inform her he had no intentions of keeping himself only unto her as he had vowed just yesterday. Oh, this was such a muddled mess.

"Sarah?" He pulled back and peered down at her. He must have sensed her withdrawal and she owed him some explanation. But was now the time to come clean? Before she had a chance to win him over?

Quinn made her choice for her. He stepped back and shoved his hands into his coat pockets. She felt bereft of his touch, but told herself it was for the best.

She, too, stepped back to put more distance between them. "Quinn, I—"

"Sarah. I'm sorry. I shouldn't have done that. At least, not yet. You've only just arrived and I'm, well, a stranger to you, not considering that your little girl—our little girl—is sleeping in the only bed in the house."

"Please, Quinn. Don't apologize. I think we were both just caught up in the moment."

He nodded and picked up his hat from the seat of the rocking chair where he had dropped it earlier. "I suppose that's all it was." A twinge of sadness hit Sarah in her heart, hearing Quinn's words. He was admitting his actions were prompted by lust and not love. Well, of course not, she admonished herself. He was a man above all else and men's hearts followed their baser needs. Didn't his visit to the woman down the street on his wedding night prove that?

"I'll go see how Eugene's doing with the prisoner. And I guess I better go explain to Reverend Tilly and his wife why we missed dinner."

Sarah's hand flew to cover her gaping mouth. "Oh my. I forgot all about dinner with the reverend. He'll think me so rude."

Quinn shook his head. "I doubt that. The reverend knows what kids are like. He has a passel of them. I'll explain what happened. Do you want me to get you something to eat? Maybe something for Becca to eat later, if she wants it?"

Tears burned Sarah's eyes. "Thank you, Quinn. You've done so much for Becca and me already. I owe you so much. "

Her husband took a step closer and lifted her quivering chin with his finger. She met those beautiful eyes of his and tried to focus amidst the tears. "I wish you wouldn't look at it like that, Sarah. I owe you just as much for agreeing to come out here in the middle of nowhere and be my wife. Let's just say we have a mutual understanding that benefits us both.

"Now, I'll be back in an hour or so. That should give you the privacy you need to prepare for bed. For the time being, we'll have to share the bed with Becca. You sleep on one side and I'll take the other. If that's alright with you, that is."

"Of course. It's the practical thing to do. Since there's just the one bed."

Sarah watched Quinn nod in agreement and leave by the back door. Alone in the semi-darkness of the little house, she breathed out a troubled sigh.

She needed to buy some time until she could figure out a way to determine if the Caldwells knew of her whereabouts. In the meantime, she would learn to be a housewife.

Sarah considered asking her friends from Charleston, but did they know any more than she? Probably not, considering they were raised in much the same fashion. Women were to be seen and not heard unless one counted decisions made regarding which fabric or color or style to direct the seamstress to sew the latest party fashion.

She had never realized how sheltered and controlled the young women of Charleston were until just this moment. Sarah had dreamed of independence, but she knew now that, had it been granted to her, she wouldn't have had even the slightest notion what to do with it.

"Quinn Cassidy. You deserve a good wife. And I vow to learn to be that wife—just as soon as I can find someone who can teach me to cook."

Quinn trudged through the icy snow down the alley to the side door of his office. It was late. He guessed around nine-thirty give or take half an hour. And, in spite of his words to Sarah about being caught up in the moment, he wished he were still wrapped in the warmth of his wife's body between those clean, cozy sheets Mrs. Lawrence had been so kind to gift him. He just wished little Becca wasn't sleeping in between them.

He reached for the office door's latch off the alley and let himself inside. Eugene was sitting in his desk chair playing solitaire with himself. The look of surprise on his deputy's face made him grin.

"Surprised to see me, are you? How's our prisoner?" Quinn closed the door behind him.

Eugene nodded in agreement. "Good, I suppose. I left a while ago to get ole' Johnny Reb's dinner but the Widda Lawrence waddunt home. I gave him half my dinner and he's still bitchin' about bein' hungry."

"I'm sorry about that, Eugene. I'm not sure why Flora wasn't home, but I know she's expecting us. I told her with the nasty turn in the weather, it may be a couple of weeks before we're relieved of our ungracious guest.

"Why don't I walk on over to the widow's and see if she made it home yet? Get you something? She had a nice pot of beef stew and homemade cornbread last night. I think I even smelled some apple pie cookin'," Quinn offered.

"Nah, I'm good. Mom packed two extra elk steaks and half a loaf of home-baked bread. Some cookies too. Can't wait to dig into those." Eugene lowered his voice to a whisper. "I didn't share none of my cookies with the prisoner though. I figure he's been bad enough he don't deserve no treats."

Quinn grinned at his deputy. "I'd say I'm in full agreement, Eugene. Full and complete agreement. Now, lock the doors behind me and I'll be back in a bit."

"Yes, sir, Sheriff Cassidy."

He pulled his collar close around his throat and tightened his wool scarf against the cold wind whistling through the snow-covered pine trees. Sometimes he wished this town was bigger, but on frigid nights like this, he was glad it was only a few yards from his office to home.

Once Sarah had time to prepare her kitchen, he would no longer have to burden Mrs. Lawrence to cook for his prisoner's meals, even though he was fairly certain the widow liked having someone to cook for, even if it was a man behind bars.

Quinn stepped up on to the boardwalk and walked under the saloon's covered porch until he reached the end. He stepped down and continued the well-worn path down the street to the house on the end with the pretty picket fence. He nodded to a couple of passersby—men headed home to their families. Not many people out this time of night—not with the temperature plummeting like it was.

Quinn shot a quick look toward his own house as he walked toward the widow's big two story house. He thought about the woman and child inside its walls waiting—for him. It gave him a contented feeling deep down in his gut. And he liked it—a lot.

He knocked on the painted white door and the widow soon appeared. "Hey there, Sheriff. Sorry I'm so late getting your prisoner's dinner. Me and Prudence Bailey got caught up in knitting Christmas presents and, well, we lost track of time. Come on in."

He nodded his greeting and entered the widow's house. It smelled of cinnamon and apples. He stood in her nice-sized living room with his hat in his hand. She closed the door behind him and headed to her kitchen in the back of the house, talking small talk along the way. "How's married life, Sheriff?"

"It's going alright. I suppose. Sarah is gonna work on setting up the house tomorrow. And just so ya know, once Sarah gets comfortable with her kitchen, I won't need to impose any more on your hospitality. I should be gettin' a check soon from the city council to pay you for all the meals I been leachin' off ya."

"No hurry about that. I'm just happy to have something to do."

"Well, just the same, I'm not one to impose."

Quinn stood in the widow's living room and looked around while she prepared the food in the kitchen. He hadn't noticed the interior of the house before. He liked its homey feel.

"Here you go, Sheriff. Tell Eugene I put some extra potato soup and fresh baked bread in there for him. An extra piece of pie too."

"Thank you, Mrs. Lawrence. Eugene said he's done had his supper, but if it's alright with you, I'll take the extra food to Sarah and Becca. We were supposed to eat with the reverend but, well, Becca kinda got upset.

"Of course, I can even put a little extra if you need more." Flora offered.

"No, I think this is plenty. I don't even know if they'll be up to eat it. I just wanted to have it there in case they did."

"You are a good husband, Mr. Cassidy. It's not easy to take on a whole family at once. "

"Yeah, it's a bit harder than I thought it would be, but it'll just take us some time to—adjust." He hoped that was all it was.

Quinn took the box of food the widow prepared and turned to go. A sudden thought stopped him. He turned back to the widow and said, "I've never really asked you before what your plans are now that your husband is gone. Do you plan to stay in Angel Creek or do you have family somewhere else?"

The woman paused for a moment and looked around the house. "You know, Sheriff. I hadn't given that much thought before last week. Now, it's been a constant thing on my mind."

"What happened last week?" The words were out of Quinn's mouth before he thought about how nosey he sounded. "If you don't mind me asking, that is?" He added.

Widow Lawrence smiled. "I don't mind. Truth is, I been living day-to-day since Walter's heart gave out all of a sudden. It's a comfort to see his things everywhere. Like he could walk in that door any minute and ask me what's for dinner."

Quinn saw the grief on the widow's face. Tears glistened in her sad blue eyes. He felt responsible for reminding her of her loss. "I'm sorry, Mrs. Lawrence, I didn't mean to bring up your memories—"

"Nonsense. I love talking about Walter and remembering. It ain't the memories that pain me. It's the being alone that eats at my soul. I never thought I'd live a day on this earth without my Walter after we married. I still expect to see my Walter sittin' in that rockin' chair over there by the fire, but when he ain't, that's when the silence of this big old house bears down on me."

The woman stopped talking and wiped her eyes with her apron. The sniffle amidst the silence in the living room made Quinn feel awful. He should have kept his mouth shut. He shuffled the box of food to his other arm. "I'm sorry, Mrs. Lawrence—"

"Nothing to apologize for, Sheriff. Thank you for asking about my Walter. Most people tiptoe around the subject. Guess they're afraid I'll have some kind of breakdown, but I'm made of stronger stock than that. Anyway, to answer your question, I hadn't thought of leavin' Angel Creek until I received a letter from my sister last week. She's beggin' me to come back to St. Louis and live with her and her husband. I just don't know what I'd do with this big old house. Walter built it with his own two hands. I'd hate to just abandon it. It'd be like leavin' an old friend."

"Well, dependin' on how much you want for it, I'd be in the market for a new house. I mean, I got a family now and that old shack I'm renting isn't really a proper place to raise a young daughter."

"Or raise a family. There's no room for more children, Sheriff. No room at all." The widow grinned at him. Her unspoken message clear. He didn't plan to share the fact with the widow he couldn't father any more children. However, he did owe that truth to his new bride. A truth he should have told her before she pledged her vows to him.

"If you do decide to go to St. Louis to live with your sister, will you give me first right of refusal on the house, Mrs. Lawrence?"

"I certainly will. If I decide to go back, you'll be the first to know. Now you get out of here or that soup is gonna be ice cold. Not fit for serving." The kindly woman shooed him out the door and into the cold dark night alone with his thoughts.

Quinn walked the short distance from the Lawrence house to the jail. A glance at his tiny house revealed the faint glow of the lamp left burning in the dark. His family lay sleeping.

He picked up his pace and headed straight to the jail, side-stepping the drifts of snow pushed off the sidewalk by shop keepers. There was nothing he wanted more than to deliver this food to his prisoner and head home. Home to his new family who waited—for *him.*

CHAPTER 9

*S*arah woke early. She heard a clock chime the hour. Five am. She never woke this early in Charleston. *Charleston.* She could admit she missed her life in that once great southern city. She missed shopping with her friends. Sharing tea with her friends. Gossiping with her friends.

She smiled in the early morning darkness. Everything she did in Charleston revolved around her dear friends—Julia, Charity, Anna and Ruby. She was so grateful they were here with her on this unusual journey. She would try to visit Charity today. Perhaps when the snow melted a bit, she could convince Quinn to take her to see Anna and Julia. She needed to know if their new lives were working out any better than hers.

She had tried to go to sleep after Quinn left the night before, but she couldn't. The feel of his lips touching hers kept her mind active and her heart racing. Finally, she put on her robe and slippers and wandered around the jumbled house avoiding stacks of rugs and dishes and curtains and, well, everything. She decided she would plan a visit with her friend Charity at the saloon very soon. She was in desperate need of advice.

It had been thoughts of her friend married to the saloon keeper that made her look out the window across the dark, evening street when she caught a glimpse of Quinn once more slipping in and out of the night shadows toward the woman's house at the end of the street.

He'd visited the mysterious woman's house at such an inappropriate hour two nights in a row. Who was she and what did she mean to Quinn? Sarah thought she knew men, but how could he be so sweet, generous and oh-so-appealing one moment, and the next traipse off into the darkness to visit *her*.

A snore close by scattered her memories of the night before into the diffused early morning light. She jumped at the unexpected noise. She turned her head and witnessed not one, but two bed partners sleeping peacefully in the pre-dawn light.

Becca's limbs were sprawled over three-quarters of the bed. It was then Sarah realized she was hugging the edge of the bed. She wondered how on earth she kept from falling to the floor. Sheer exhaustion had prevented her from moving a muscle she supposed.

Another loud snore pulled her thoughts, and her eyes, to her other bed partner. Sometime after he left the other woman's house, Quinn must have decided to walk his unfaithful-self home and put himself to bed. In her bed. *The nerve.*

A wave of guilt washed away her ire. She had firsthand experience that married men didn't stay faithful. It must have been a part of their nature they had no control over. It was certainly true in William's case. She had hoped Quinn would be different.

Quinn snored again. She had to admit, his presence in the bed made her feel safe and protected. And he swore he would provide for her and Becca. Did she have a right to demand more?

Sarah propped her head in her cupped palm and bent her elbow into her pillow. This was the perfect opportunity to study her handsome sleeping husband.

He slept in his long underwear. Sarah knew he had done it out of respect for Becca. She was coming to know he was a considerate man even as he stole away after dark to spend time with another woman. *Husbands.*

The gentle rise and fall of his wide chest under the blankets had her thinking about their kiss. Her heart stumbled at the memory of his arms wrapped around her body. She closed her eyes and remembered the feel of Quinn's hard chest muscles against her cheek. She allowed her mind to wander, unfettered, over Quinn's body. She remembered how his arm muscles bunched and relaxed when he held her tight against his hard body.

And then there was that bulge. The one she'd felt between them through their clothing. The one south of the waistband of his jeans. It was obvious he was attracted to her. And she to him. Very much so.

She stared at the spot hidden underneath the covers. Would it be so wrong of her to seduce her own husband? Would it even work? She had tried it with William when she found out about his indiscretions, but to no avail. Perhaps she wasn't the kind of woman men would stay loyal to, but she was certain she would like to—

"Sarah, I swear. If you keep looking at me like that, Becca will be sleeping on the kitchen table."

Startled by the sound of Quinn's whisper in the gray morning light, her face heated with embarrassment. Dear

Lord. Had she been so deep in her inappropriate thoughts, she hadn't noticed Quinn was awake? What should she say now?

"I—was looking in your direction, I suppose. I was thinking, you know, in an absent-minded way. That's all. I have so much to do today." Her calm words were at odds with the blazing blush she felt stain her cheeks. She knew Quinn saw her excuse for what it was, but, thankfully, he gifted her with that devastating smile of his and let the subject go.

Becca stirred between them. Quinn watched her daughter's eyes open. Her bottom lip puckered when she surveyed her surroundings. "I wanna go home." Tears formed in Becca's blue eyes. "I. Wanna. Go. Hooooome!"

Sarah was at her wit's end with her daughter's outbursts. She understood and empathized with Becca's losses. She felt them too. But enough was enough. Before Sarah could rein in her daughter's latest tempest, Quinn interceded.

"But, Becca. If you go back to Charleston, you won't get to help decorate your new bedroom or make new friends at your new school. But most important of all, you won't get to ride in Mr. Willie's sleigh into the forest to cut down our very own Christmas tree. And you know, without the tree, Santa might not know how to find you. And, if he can't find you, how will you get your gifts?"

Sarah could see her daughter pondering Quinn's words. She knew there was a chance, a small chance, that Becca might give some credence to the truth of what Quinn said. Living three months underneath the roof of William's parents had made her daughter a little bit self-absorbed. Mercenary would be a better word choice.

Those two had done everything they could, used every conniving trick they possessed, to turn Becca from her. And, to some degree, it had worked. Now, it was up to Sarah to reacclimate her daughter to the finer points of generosity and charitable acts.

"Is that true, Momma? Will Santa leave my presents here if I go back to Charleston before Christmas?" Becca's clear blue eyes pinned her with doubt and demanded an answer.

"Becca, I am almost one hundred percent certain, if you were to leave for Charleston now, you would not arrive until well after Christmas, and any presents Santa has for you would, in fact, be delivered here—in Angel Creek."

Becca looked back and forth between her and Quinn. Sarah could tell he struggled to keep a straight face, but he managed somehow. She remained serious as well.

Finally, her daughter seemed to come to some type of understanding of the situation inside her own little six-year-old head. "Very well, then. If Santa is going to visit me here, then we must get the tree ready. When can we cut our tree, Quinn?" Becca crossed her arms and left Quinn no room to back track. But as it turned out, Becca's new father had no intention of letting his little girl down.

"Well, we don't want to cut it too soon or it will dry out before Christmas, but we can go pick one out. How about I check to see when my prisoner is leaving us? And if that doesn't happen in time to get the tree, then I'll check around town to see if someone can come in and watch him while we go look for the perfect tree. How does that sound?"

Both Becca and Sarah nodded in agreement. Sarah watched the pleased look on her husband's face. He was so excited to give them a good Christmas.

"We can take the sleigh and ride out to Otto Schultz's sawmill if the weather's nice. Then, maybe your momma will pack us a hot meal in a picnic basket and we can even skate on Otto's pond, if it's iced over enough, that is."

Quinn reached over and tweaked Becca's nose. Sarah heard her daughter's giggle and it would have done her mother's heart good—if she hadn't been so rattled about the thought of cooking again. She watched Quinn tickle Becca and the little girl kicked and laughed in delight.

He sent her a heated look before he rolled out of bed, careful to cover himself in front of Becca. Woolen underwear alone couldn't hide a grown man's...assets. Not when those assets were full of anticipation. "I'll get dressed in the front room."

He turned and left the bedroom, leaving Sarah with her riotous thoughts. A moment later, fully dressed, he stuck his head inside the bedroom door where she and Becca still cozied beneath the warm blankets. "I'm gonna check on Eugene and the prisoner. I'll be back in about an hour or so for breakfast. I'm starving."

Quinn's innocent declaration sent chills of trepidation through Sarah even the stack of warm blankets couldn't hold at bay. "Breakfast? Um...sure. We'll be ready," she stammered.

The breath-stealing smile her husband gifted her with made her wish preparing him breakfast were as simple as getting dressed and making her way to the kitchen. But it wasn't, and she wasn't certain what she was going to do about it.

Quinn whistled a random Christmas song to himself during the short walk to his office. Things were looking up. Sarah was most definitely attracted to him. He came close to losing all self-control when he awoke that morning to find her looking at him in that way a woman did when she wanted a man. And he was delighted to oblige his wife—as soon as she gave him the sign she was ready.

Becca was a pleasant surprise that morning as well. Her initial outburst had him searching for something to win her over. He didn't know how the idea of a Christmas tree and presents came to mind, but he was glad it did. Besides, what little girl wouldn't succumb to the wonder of the Christmas season. He was a grown man and he loved everything about this time of year. He would spend every dime he possessed to make it the most wonderful Christmas Becca had in all of her six years on this earth.

He walked between the apothecary-bath house building and around to the boardwalk in front of the jail. He peeked inside the office window and saw Eugene playing cards with himself again.

Quinn pecked on the window to get Eugene's attention. He twisted the front door handle and stepped inside. "Good morning, Deputy. Everything all quiet with our prisoner?"

Eugene stood and stretched his long, lanky frame. "Yep. Ain't heard nothin' out of the man except he's hungry. Don't they feed people down south none? He ain't nothin' but one big ole' holler leg."

Quinn laughed at Eugene's observation. "The war was mighty hard on a lot of folks. Maybe he just doesn't trust yet where his next meal's comin' from."

"Well, he's gonna know soon," Eugene said. "When the judge sends him to prison for the next ten years, that oughta calm down his bottomless stomach. Ain't never heard of no prison with food to recommend, that's for sure."

"I expect you are right about that, Deputy Phillips. Now, I'm gonna take a turn around town. Make sure everybody's behavin'. Sarah should have breakfast ready by then. I'll grab a bite and then be back with ole' Johnny Reb's breakfast, say around six forty-five—seven at the latest."

Eugene nodded and poured himself a cup of coffee. "Sounds good, Sheriff."

He checked on the prisoner. Johnny was still snoozing in

his bunk. Good. He hoped the man would sleep in. He sure was a pesky sort, always complaining about something.

Quinn nodded to Eugene on his way out the front door and closed it behind him. He decided he sure was lucky to have found such a reliable deputy. Made his lot in life easier. He could spend his evenings and nights with his family, now that he had one.

He smiled to himself at the memory of waking up with two women in his bed. One giggled when he tickled her. The other sent him looks that made him want to lock the first one out of the bedroom. Better yet, Becca needed her own bedroom to sleep in. He hoped Sarah made that her first domestic priority. That and setting the kitchen to rights.

Quinn strolled around Angel Creek in the early morning hours of the crisp November day. It was early, but the sky was clear. It promised to be sunny and a bit warmer. He hoped the temperatures would rise to at least above freezing, but it was hard to predict how cold it would get in Montana Territory this time of year.

He poked his head inside the blacksmith's shop. "Hey there. How's it goin'?" In spite of the cold morning, the blacksmith was sweating from the intense heat of his bellows.

"Good, Sheriff. You?"

Quinn never could get more than a few words at a time from the blacksmith. Today was no exception.

"No complaints," Quinn said. The burly man nodded and raised his hammer to his anvil again. The incessant strikes rang in Quinn's ears and made it crystal clear the man didn't want to talk any more. "Well, I'll finish my rounds. Just wanted to stick my head in and say hey. Might need some shoes put on ole' Jack in a week or so. Will you have time?"

"Sure thing, Sheriff. Bring 'im on by anytime." That was all the man said before he turned back to his work.

Quinn left the blacksmith hard at work and walked back

across the snowy street to the stables, past the boarding house, Oliver's restaurant and finally the stage coach office which was closed until further notice because of the weather. No stages in or out for the foreseeable future, which made him wonder how that heavy prison wagon was gonna get through. It didn't look likely his prisoner was leaving any time soon.

The aroma coming from Mr. Oliver's restaurant made his empty belly rumble loud enough to be heard from underneath his heavy coat. Maybe he felt it more than heard it, but it reminded him he was due home for breakfast.

Quinn turned away from the tantalizing aromas and walked across the street and over by the corral where he and Eugene kept their horses when on duty. He passed the apothecary/bath house building and stopped at the back door of his own little home. He did like the sound of that word.

Brushing the snow off his boots, he entered the little store room leading to the kitchen door and sat on the wooden bench to remove his wet boots. He shoved them under the bench and removed his coat, hooking it on a peg on the wall above the bench.

Sock footed he opened the back door to the kitchen and stopped in stunned silence. Where was breakfast? Where was the woman who was supposed to be cooking breakfast? He listened for sounds to indicate where she was. Nothing.

Everything was as it had been that morning. Pots and pans hung on the wall next to the stove. Wood that should have been used to heat the stove to cook his breakfast was still stacked neatly against the wall. Even the box of food Flora Lawrence had given him for supper last night. Still sitting right where he had left it.

His stunned gaze scanned the neat and empty kitchen for

signs of an explanation. Eugene was waiting on him. And his prisoner wanted breakfast.

It was then he spied a small hand-written note leaning upright against a flour canister on the top shelf of the dough board. Quinn shuffled in sock-covered feet to it, lifting it so he could read the neat cursive words on the page.

"Dearest Quinn: I was preparing for your breakfast, and ours, when I discovered there was not an adequate amount of leavening ingredients for the biscuits. In my opinion, there's nothing worse than a flat biscuit. Don't you agree? Since the mercantile isn't yet open, Becca and I have gone for breakfast at Mr. Oliver's restaurant. If you get this note in time, we would be so pleased if you came to join us." Sarah

Quinn stared at the note in his hand for a full minute. How could there not be enough baking soda for biscuits? He had just bought a full tin last week in preparation for his new bride. He hadn't used but a dash or two since then.

The tin was sitting on the dough board. Out of curiosity he pulled the lid and looked inside. Yep. The tin was empty. That was so odd. He knew it was nearly full just last week. He replaced the lid on the tin and set it up on the shelf. No point in stewing over it. His family was eating breakfast without him. And, his prisoner was gonna be belly aching soon, not to mention Eugene needed to head home and get some rest. For two cents, he'd take the cold potato soup to Johnny Bishop, but he knew the man would whine all day about his mistreatment of not having breakfast at breakfast. The man was a real pain in his back side. He would let Flora know he still had need of her services for three squares until Sarah was able to get the kitchen stocked, he hoped by the end of the day. Flora would have something on hand since she cooked for just about everyone around town that needed help.

He'd go by Flora's house and get what he could. Guess he

owed Eugene an apology too for making him work past his shift. Couldn't be helped.

Quinn shoved the note in his jean pocket and left the cold kitchen. He retraced his steps to the outer room and put on his boots and coat. The sun was just peeking over the mountains when he stepped outside into the snow and rounded the corner of his house on his way to the widow's.

Maybe he would buy Sarah a new fancy stove like the one he had seen in the mercantile window when he was there yesterday. All brass and cast iron and big enough to cook for twenty people. It was a beauty. Or, even better than a new stove would be a whole new house. One more fitting of a woman like Sarah.

Quinn rounded the corner of his house and walked down the boardwalk toward the Widow Lawrence's house. There it stood at the end of the street. Solid. Dependable. Welcoming. It was the perfect house.

He could imagine Becca playing inside the white picket fence with her dog, laughing and running around like a six-year old girl should be doing.

He walked down the boardwalk to the house and stood in front of it. His eyes took in the sweep of the covered porch across the front of the grand old place. He imagined Sarah sitting in one of the wood rockers, he in the other, watching Becca play in the yard. He studied the curve of the arched stained glass window on the second floor. He knew that window rose above the second story landing.

He fantasized about the biggest Christmas tree standing in front of the tall bay window, its beautiful fragrant boughs aglitter with tin and glass ornaments, colorful candies, and toys for Becca. For the first time since his parents died and his brothers were killed in the war, he was looking forward to Christmas.

The Widow Lawrence called out to him from her front

porch. Deep in thought, he hadn't seen the woman come out of the house wrapped in a heavy shawl. "Sheriff? You been standing out there in the cold staring at the house for a while now. Are you okay?"

Quinn grinned. "Yes, ma'am. I've never been better."

CHAPTER 10

*S*arah's guilt weighed on her conscious. She cut another anxious look toward the front door of Mr. Oliver's restaurant. Would Quinn see the note and join her? She hoped he would, but then again—

She wrung her fingers in her napkin under the white tablecloth. Quinn was handsome and very well respected around town. He deserved a good wife. The kind of wife who didn't keep secrets from her husband.

"Momma, I'm hungry. Are we going to order soon?" Becca squirmed in her chair and picked at the edge of the napkin lying in her lap.

Sarah looked toward the entrance once more, hoping to see Quinn walking through the door with that alluring smile of his pointed in her direction. Where could he be? Perhaps he hadn't finished his rounds. Or, what if he hadn't seen the note?

A sudden thought punched her in the chest. What if he had seen the note and knew what she had done with the nearly full tin of baking soda? She hadn't thought this plan through when she dumped the contents of the tin out into the snow and covered it up to hide her crime. No, he couldn't possibly know. Could He? Oh, this wasn't going at all the way she had hoped. Not. At. All.

"Momma!" Becca's volume increased with her hunger. Several of the patrons turned to stare at them.

"Becca. A proper lady doesn't screech in public. Please lower your voice. Yes, we will order as soon as Quinn arrives. Don't you want to wait on Quinn?" Sarah pleaded, nodding and smiling to some of the ladies still glaring in her direction. Did none of them have a six-year-old at home?

Sarah checked the front door once more. No sign of Quinn. She took a deep breath and signaled to the waitress that they were ready to place their order.

Less than an hour later, Sarah paid her check and stood to leave. She gathered her belongings and wrapped Becca up in warm scarfs, a heavy wool coat, mittens and rabbit fur-lined ear muffs. Her daughter could barely move. Sarah felt silly. After all, it was only a half a block home.

She needed to stop by the mercantile on the way home to replace the leavening she dumped in the snow. What excuse was she going to use next for not cooking her husband's meals?

Lost in her troubled thoughts, she collided with a woman at the door.

The attractive older woman apologized immediately. "I'm so sorry, my dear. I was in such a hurry, I didn't even look where I was going. Please forgive me." The woman's pleasant voice was soothing. She reminded Sarah of her own mother.

"It was entirely my fault, ma'am. I was lost in my own thoughts and wasn't looking where I was walking," Sarah offered.

The woman peered down at Becca and smiled. "And who is this little lady? What beautiful blue eyes you have. What is your name, my dear?" The woman bent down to Becca's level.

Becca stepped up and answered loud and clear. "My name is Rebecca. What's yours?"

The lady smiled. "My name is Flora Lawrence. I don't believe I've seen you two in town before. Are you new here?"

Before Sarah could answer, Becca spoke up, her expression showed her displeasure. "Yes, we *used* to live in Charleston, but now we have to live *here*."

The woman shook her head in understanding. "I see. Well, that explains why you aren't in school today. If you haven't had a chance to meet your teacher, her name is Mrs. Schultz. She is a lovely woman and her students have the best time in her classroom."

"I don't want to go to school here. I want to go back to my school in Charleston—" Becca's voice rose another notch.

Sarah grabbed Becca's hand and started to usher her out the door when the waitress joined them at the door. "Good morning, Flora. Are you here for your order?" the young woman asked.

"Yes, I am. And could you please ask the cook to add a few more slices of crisp bacon and biscuits? It wasn't on my original order, but I have a hungry man on my hands this morning I hadn't expected."

The waitress nodded and turned to do the woman's request. Sarah wondered why a woman of a certain age would need to order food. Perhaps Sarah wasn't the only woman in this town who didn't know how to cook.

"I suppose your stove is out of commission this morning to be ordering so much food for your family," Sarah asked as innocently as she could.

The woman laughed out loud. It was a very nice sound and Sarah found herself warming up to the lady. "No, not at all." Sarah noticed a sad look in the woman's eyes. *Oh, no. I've said something wrong.* Before she had a chance to apologize, the lady offered an explanation.

"I'm widowed. My dear husband, Walter, passed away this past summer. The doctor said it was his heart. It just gave out."

Sarah felt horrible for causing this nice woman an ounce of pain. Sarah reached out and touched her arm to console her. "I'm so sorry for your loss. And I'm doubly sorry for causing you pain by making you relive that moment. My deep and sincere apologies, ma'am."

The woman's kind eyes held the glitter of unshed tears. "Nonsense. I love talking about Walter. He was my heart and soul for over twenty-two years. I don't want to ever forget him, the dear, sweet man."

"Do you have children then? They must be a comfort for you now that your husband is gone." Sarah offered.

"No, we had no children. They just—never came."

Sarah was now positively mortified. She knew she should probably just keep her mouth shut and stop asking questions.

"Please don't look so distressed," the woman consoled her. "I'm happy with the life God blessed me with. You'll not hear me complain one bit. And to answer your question about my stove, no it isn't broken. I cook most every morning. I have an arrangement with several businesses in town to provide food for one reason or another and I cook extra to give to those who aren't as blessed as I am. However, this morning, I had a request for food I wasn't expecting so I'm getting a little extra help from Mr. Oliver's kitchen."

A spark lit in Sarah's brain. This woman could cook. And she must be good if people were willing to pay her for her food. Sarah wondered if she'd be willing to teach her. The thought shot a bright glimmer of possibility through Sarah's despair.

The waitress returned with the woman's food. "Here you

go, Flora. If you need any more, cook said to let him know by ten o'clock."

"I will do that, Myrna." The woman turned toward her struggling to balance her boxes of food and a large cloth sack.

"It was very nice to meet you both. I hope to see you around town again very soon. Perhaps you would like to join some of us ladies in the sewing circle group. We eat potluck food and drink wassail and knit or crochet or sew gifts for the needy. We have a big gift basket every year we put under the tree at the Christmas Eve party for those less fortunate. You did say you were new in town, right?"

Sarah's mind was working hard. She needed to ask this lady to teach her to cook but, could the woman be trusted not to gossip the truth all over town?

"Yes, we are new in town. Let me help you with all that food. I can give you a hand to carry it if you would like," Sarah offered. Helping the woman would, at the very least, give her a little more time to speak with her about the possibility of cooking lessons.

"Oh, that would be so kind of you. I could use the help, if it wouldn't be an imposition for you."

Sarah breathed a sigh of relief. "Of course not. It would be my pleasure." The woman handed her the larger box she was holding and readjusted the smaller one, so she could grab the cloth sack sitting on the floor.

"I'm not going far at all. Only two blocks over. Thank you so much for your kind help. I don't think I caught your name."

"Sarah Caldwell." Sarah said her name without even thinking. And once it was out, it felt too awkward to add Quinn's last name without a lot more explaining than she wanted to do standing at the front door of Mr. Oliver's restaurant. If things worked out as Sarah hoped, she could have ample opportunity to correct the misunderstanding during her cooking lessons.

The lady nodded her head in greeting. "Well it is my pleasure to meet you both, Sarah and Rebecca. Shall we get going?"

Sarah followed the woman through the eatery door and out to the boardwalk. Becca walked close behind them. Sarah didn't know how far the woman was going, but she said it wasn't far, so Sarah needed to work up her courage and quickly. She moved beside Flora's careful footsteps in the snow.

"Mrs. Lawrence—" Sarah began.

"Please, call me Flora." Her companion insisted.

"Very well, Flora." Sarah pushed on. "I was thinking. You said you cook a lot for other business and those in need. That is a wonderful thing to do for this community. And, since I'm new in town, it might be a nice way to meet people. You know, learn to cook new dishes. Would it be alright with you if I—"

The woman turned to Sarah and grinned excitedly. "Are you offering to help me cook? Oh, that would be wonderful. I've been wanting to find someone to help me bake my famous cinnamon rolls."

Bake? Cinnamon rolls? Sarah cringed. She didn't know the first thing about how to cook an egg. How on earth would she be able to bake a pastry? Oh, this wasn't going well at all.

Lost in her troubled thoughts as she followed Flora through town, Sarah suddenly found herself standing in front of the two-story house at the end of the street. The one with the beautiful white picket fence around it. The one her husband disappeared into for the last two nights in a row.

"Wh—what are we doing *here*?" Sarah stammered.

"This is where I live." Flora stepped inside, and Becca

followed leaving Sarah standing on the front porch considering her options and none were very appealing. She could drop the food where she stood, pull her daughter out of that harlot's house, and march out the gate and down the street to her own house.

Or she could step inside the house and demand to know why this woman was carrying on with her husband behind her back—in front of Becca. Her mind was a tangled mess of shock, disbelief and growing indignation.

Sarah weighed her options and decided a full out brawl on the front lawn with her daughter watching wasn't an option. So, she stepped inside the house and followed the woman to the kitchen where they deposited all the food. Now what?

It was all so disappointing. She liked the woman. She seemed so nice, but then again so had her friend, Caroline Murdoch, until Sarah found out she was the devious husband-stealing tramp who was sleeping with William behind her back.

And another fact to consider—Sarah was new in town and she was certain Flora was a well-respected pillar of the community if all the cooking and sewing and caring for the needy was any indication. Who would take her side?

How would Quinn react to her confrontation with his mistress? William's response had been cold and condescending. She didn't know Quinn well enough to have any clue into his true nature. He seemed nice enough, but he had a mistress—and he had paid her a visit on Sarah's wedding night. Could this situation get any worse?

A loud knock at the door startled her.

"Just in time. He's here. Becca, dear. How would you like to taste one of my famous cinnamon rolls?"

Sarah stood in the roomy parlor undecided whether she should stay or go when Becca pulled on her skirt. "Momma, the lady said I could have a cinnamum roll. Can I, Momma?" Before Sarah could form her response, Flora opened the door and invited her guest inside.

"Ah, Flora, I came by earlier, but you weren't at home. I am about near starved to death—"

It was then Sarah saw *her husband* 's shock of recognition when he noticed her and Becca standing in the Jezebel's living room. His shocked look might have been comical under other circumstances. But she didn't think anything about this situation was funny.

Flora stood back and motioned her husband inside. She eyed them both with a curious stare. "You know Sheriff Cassidy?" she asked Sarah.

What should she say? *Yes, of course, I know him. He's my husband.* Or perhaps, *you mean this man, the one you've been cavorting with behind his wife's back?*

Before Sarah's brain could form a rational response, Quinn spoke up and admitted his guilt. "Yes, Flora. Sarah and I do know each other. Please allow me to make the introductions. Sarah, this is the Widow Lawrence. Flora, this is Sarah, the bride I ordered from Charleston."

CHAPTER 11

*I*t was a bit disconcerting to be introduced as the bride he ordered. In fact, it was humiliating even though it was the truth down to the letter.

Sarah had to give the man credit. It wasn't everyday a cheating husband had the gall, the courage, the nerve, to introduce his wife to his mistress. And she had to admit, the widow was taking it quite well herself.

Perhaps Quinn wasn't the only married man this woman entertained. She would have to make certain Charity watched her husband, Lewis. The saloon was only two doors down from the black widow's web. And then there was Ruby. She would warn Ruby too, when she and her husband got back from their trip. Why, the doctor's house was right next door. Barely ten feet away from this harlot's door. *How convenient.*

"Come in, Sheriff. Let's get you some food and then we can discuss our arrangement. Since you have a wife now, I imagine your needs have changed."

Sarah couldn't believe her ears. The two of them were discussing their rendezvous right in front of her. Right in front of Becca. Is that what they did here in the west? Was there no respect for the sanctity of marriage? No common decency among women? How dare these two—

"Sarah? Are you going to sit down?" She blinked away images of Flora and Quinn locked in a lover's embrace and instead saw Quinn sitting at the woman's dining room table.

"I hardly think that would be appropriate, considering—"

The widow countered. "Nonsense. Please come join us. We have much to talk about now that we know about each other."

Sarah's mind reeled. *This can't be happening.* At least William had the decency to act offended when she found out about his affair. Quinn was sitting at the woman's table having breakfast. And he was expecting her to join them. Well, she had never heard of such goings on. It was barbaric.

"Didn't you say your name was Caldwell, Sarah? Becca. Would you like a cinnamon roll?" Flora offered. Well that was just too much. Now the woman was trying to win over her daughter? *I won't have it.*

"No. Thank you, Mrs. Lawrence. She just ate breakfast and yes, I did introduce myself as Caldwell. I'm not used to my new name yet. I'm a widow—"

"I want one!" Becca demanded. Without waiting for help from Sarah, her daughter climbed up into the chair next to Quin. He scooted her chair under the table and Flora dug into the pan of the sticky pastries.

Sarah supposed the next step was to do away with her and bury her body on the frozen mountain somewhere. Now she was just being ridiculous. The ground was too frozen to bury a body—

"Come join us, Sarah. We have a lot to talk about." Quinn stood and pulled out the chair on his other side for her. What should she do?

Quinn was still standing, waiting for her to take the chair

he offered, a look of puzzlement on his face at her hesitation. Were men so thick headed they had no clue a wife would find it insulting to share her bed with another woman? Awareness dawned on Sarah. He didn't know she knew about the other woman.

She took the chair Quinn offered, refusing to meet his eyes. She would wait for her husband to start the conversation. Would he pretend there was nothing amiss?

After William's affair with Carolyn, she threatened to leave him, but when he called her bluff, she realized she had no place else to go. She was at the mercy of her husband. Was her situation now any different? She was thousands of miles from her home in Charleston, and even if she could go home, William's parents were waiting to take Becca away from her again and have her arrested for kidnapping her own child.

Quinn spoke, his words punching through her indignation and worry. "Sarah, I'm sorry I missed you at breakfast. I found your note, but once I realized you couldn't cook breakfast this morning, I had to get over here to Flora as soon as I could." She watched her husband cast a fond gaze toward the other woman. How dare he make google eyes at her in front of his own wife. A wife he vowed to honor less than twenty-four hours ago. "I can always count on Flora here to help a fella out."

Sarah's face pinked with embarrassment. She couldn't believe her ears. He was admitting his guilt.

Flora rounded the table with a fresh pot of coffee and filled their cups. She placed a cold glass of milk next to Becca and sat back down at the table. "Sheriff, your wife has graciously volunteered to help me cook for some of the less fortunate. That was very sweet of her, don't you think, considering she just arrived in town?"

She watched in disbelief as Quinn and Becca merrily stuffed their mouths with the woman's cinnamon rolls. She could admit the aroma of cinnamon, butter and sugar permeated the beautiful home. It was all beautiful except for the ugly truth that hung in the air between them.

Her husband shot a surprised look in her direction. "I think that's a wonderful gesture, Sarah. Thank you for your offer. I know everyone in Angel Creek will come to appreciate your cookin' as much as they do Flora's." He winked at her in that teasing way of his. Her traitorous heart bucked at the sight of her handsome husband flirting with her. *In front of the other woman. Remember that, Sarah. He can't be trusted.*

"As soon as you get that little diamond-in-the-rough house of ours fixed up, I would be willing to share you with the Widow Lawrence here a few times a week." Her husband turned to the other woman. "Would that suit your needs, Flora?"

Sarah's face heated. Her husband was going to share *her* with his mistress? A few times a week? She couldn't sit still any longer. She didn't know what she was going to do, but she wouldn't tolerate this travesty of a marriage a minute longer. Not. One. Minute. Longer.

"How dare you say that to me. I won't stand for this sort of behavior any longer. Becca and I are leaving."

Becca whined, "But I don't want to leave. I want to stay and have more cinnamum rolls."

She pulled Becca out of her chair and unceremoniously wrapped her in her coat and pulled her out the door, slamming it behind her with a mighty surge of anger. She wished the sound gave her more gratification, but the truth was she felt humiliated. And very much afraid.

What was she going to do, where could she go, now that she had crossed the line of no return? Would Quinn be amicable to ceasing this unholy tryst with this woman or would he shrug his shoulders and tell her to take it or leave it as William had done? Dear Lord, what would she do if he did?

~

Quinn sat staring at the door Sarah had slammed shut in her furious wake. He turned to the widow and threw up his hands. "What was that all about?"

Flora cleared the dishes from the table and smiled. "Sheriff Cassidy, you and that beautiful wife of yours have only been married a couple of days. It takes some time to get to know each other and since you and Sarah married the moment you met, it's safe to say neither of you have a clear understanding of the other's needs.

"By your wife's reaction, perhaps she wasn't seeking your permission to cook alongside me. Just maybe she is an independent woman who is used to making her own decisions. Or, could it be her history is more troubling that that? What do you know about her past? I think you owe your new wife a smidgeon of curiosity about who she is, don't you?"

"Maybe. I'll admit I don't know much. Nothing more than what I could get out of the newspaper that posted the advertisements. I know she and her daughter have had a time of it because of the war. She's a confederate widow and is still coming to grips with everything that has happened because of it."

Flora nodded in understanding. "It's not easy for a woman to be left behind to carry the load when a husband dies. Whatever made her decide to leave her home and travel all this way to marry a man she had never laid eyes on, must have been pretty serious, don't you think, Sheriff?"

Quinn's heart slammed against his ribs. He was such an idiot. He had never once asked Sarah anything about her past. Did he think she just showed up never having lived one day before she arrived in Angel Creek? Flora was right. He owed his marriage a chance to succeed and the only way that might happen was if he and Sarah got to know each other.

Quinn stood for a moment soaking in the widow's words. "Perhaps you have something. I think my wife and I need to have a heart to heart talk. Would you be available to watch Becca for a few hours this evening? It's hard to speak from the heart when there are little ears about."

"Of course. I'd be delighted to spend time with your new little daughter. She seems like such a dear."

Quinn grinned. "She can be a little tart sometimes, like a green apple, but she does have her moments of sweetness too. She's had a hard time of it. They both have and I'm doin' my best to make this their best Christmas ever. Now, I have to get back to the office and check on my prisoner."

"I've got his food all packed up and ready to go." Flora disappeared into her kitchen and returned with a cloth sack. "Be patient, Sheriff. The Christmas season is the perfect time to show those two how much they mean to you, don't you think?"

Quinn nodded in agreement. "You might have something there, Flora. You just might have something there."

He wished he had time to stop by the house and check on his wife. Sarah had been so angry when she flew out of Flora's house. But he had a job to do and Eugene was still waiting on him to come back to the office and take over, so he could get some sleep. Maybe the time and space of a good day's work between them would give them both time to think.

Quinn crossed the snow-packed street, dodging a freight wagon and a couple of mounted riders. The sky was clear, cloudless and cerulean blue. Another beautiful November day in the mountains. Cold. Crisp. Clean. Just the way he liked it.

A quick glance in the direction of his house revealed his wife's presence at the window. The moment she saw him, she pulled the curtains back in place to shut him out. That was fine for now, but he hoped after they talked, she wouldn't be so...prickly. He liked her better when she was all soft and warm and melting beneath his kisses.

Quinn arrived back at the office and sent Eugene home to get some sleep. He stepped inside the cell area. His prisoner was sitting on his bunk, flipping a deck of cards over onto the floor.

"Here's your breakfast, Bishop. Stand back in the corner." Quinn clamped the top of the cloth sack between his side and arm while he held his gun on the prisoner and unlocked the door. He set the sack on the floor and then stepped back and relocked the cell door. He couldn't be too careful with this man. He came across as nice, but Quinn knew better. The federal marshal had given him all the details of the man's crimes.

"It's about time, Sheriff." The man grabbed the sack and spread its contents across the bed in front of him.

"More than you deserve, Bishop. Now eat." Quinn left the man busy with his food and partially closed the door between his office and the cell area. He'd wait until this evening to deposit Becca with Flora, then he and his beautiful bride would have that talk they should have had the first night of their marriage.

Four hours later, Quinn fed his prisoner lunch and locked the door between the cells and his office. Then he grabbed his coat, hat and gloves and stepped outside into the beautiful bright day.

Quinn locked his front office door behind him and pocketed the key. He pulled his lungs full of the clean mountain air and let it out slow and steady. The stress of the last few days gave him an itch he needed to scratch. And that was exactly what he was gonna do.

He walked off the boardwalk in front of his office, across the street and down the block to the stables. Nothing cleared a man's mind more than a good, solid ride through this beautiful countryside. And nothing would please him more than taking that ride on ole' Jack.

He stepped inside the dark interior of the stables. The tangy smell reminded him of his family's home back in New York on the Hudson River. A pang of homesickness stabbed him in the gut. He missed his parents. They were both long gone, and he was grateful they hadn't lived to see his two brothers killed in that despicable war.

His brothers. The thought of them pained him down deep where he kept those memories buried. It was hard to believe it had been almost two years since they had been killed. Colin died on some nameless battlefield. Two months later, he got the news Kaleb had been ambushed and badly injured while on patrol. Quinn still felt guilty that he hadn't been able to visit Kaleb before he died of infection from the amputation of his right arm.

He understood Sarah's pain and he sympathized with her loss. He truly did. But she wasn't the only one who had suffered heart-wrenching losses. That was their past and it didn't have to define their future.

"Hello, Quinn. I didn't expect to see you today."

Lost deep in his thoughts, Quinn hadn't seen Willie Albertson, the owner of the stable, walk toward him down the center aisle, pitchfork in hand.

"Hey, Willie. To tell the truth, I wasn't planning on being here, but ole Jack is calling me out for a ride. How's he been doin'?" Quinn walked to the end of the stable row. Jack already knew he was in the barn and greeted Quinn with a loud whinny.

He walked to the stall gate where Jack's head peered over at him. Quinn rubbed the blue roan's soft nose and grinned. "Hello, boy. How's the grub around here? Ole' Willie keepin' you comfortable?" The horse's large head bobbed up and down as if answering his question.

Willie came to stand next to Quinn. "That's a fine horse ya got there, Quinn. I don't suppose you'd ever consider selling him, would you?"

Quinn shook his head. "No, Willie. He saved my hide more than once during the war. I know that sounds silly and all, but we survived the war together when we probably shouldn't have. I owe him my life."

Willie nodded his understanding and spit a brown spot of chewing tobacco among the straw and manure on the dirt floor. "I get it. Had me a mule like that once. Sure do miss 'im. Died of old age, that one. Where ya headed?"

"I'm riding out to Matt Bailey's place to check on him and his new bride. His sister, Prudence, came by my office yesterday and told my deputy Matt was missing a couple of calves. She said he saw signs of wolf tracks in the area."

"Maybe they is getting more aggressive with winter settin' in." Willie picked up his pitchfork. "Well, gotta go clean me some stalls. This manure ain't gonna rake itself. If you ever change your mind on selling that horse, I got a buyer. And he'll pay good money too."

"Thanks, Willie. I won't, but if I do, I'll let you know." Quinn assured him although he knew it was a hollow promise. He would never sell Jack.

"See ya, Sheriff. " The little man walked away and disappeared inside one of the stalls. Quinn opened Jack's stall and grabbed a brush off a wooden peg outside the stall wall. He brushed Jack's iron gray coat until it glistened in the dim light of the dusky stable interior.

He pounded his long-unused horse blanket until the dust

stopped dancing in the slivers of light filtering through the tiny spaces between the wall boards. Satisfied the blanket was spotless, he centered the blanket and saddle over Jack's back and cinched them tight.

Quinn pulled Jack's bridle off the peg outside Jack's stall and cupped the bit in his hand for a minute to warm it before he slipped it into Jack's mouth, looping the top straps over his horse's twitching ears.

"Come on, boy," he murmured to the horse. "Let's work out some tension with a good long ride. How about it?"

Jack let out an ear-splitting whinny to say, "what took you so long?" Quinn laughed and walked the thick chested iron gray horse into the bright sunshine outside. The scars running over the horse's muscled rump and down his left rear leg matched Quinn's. Why shouldn't they? Both he and Quinn were nearly killed by the same cannon blast. Thank goodness his corporal knew what Jack meant to him. While Quinn was fighting for his life in the hospital, his corporal was fighting for Jack's.

He checked the cinch on Jack's saddle once more and then stepped his left foot into the stirrup and swung his other leg over his horse. It felt good to be back in the saddle. He hadn't realized how much he missed it. "We need to do this at least once a week, Jack. Maybe more if I can work it in between my job and my new family. I can't wait for you to meet them."

Quinn settled deep in the saddle and urged Jack forward, guiding him down Main Street toward Matt Bailey's place. He deliberately walked Jack down the street in front of his house hoping to catch a glimpse of his angry wife.

He wished he could ask her to ride with him. Perhaps, after they cleared the air between them, it would be a possibility. He prayed it would. He couldn't wait until summer returned to share this beautiful mountain and surrounding countryside with Sarah and Becca.

Reining Jack to a stop just outside his house, he caught sight of little Becca sitting in the front window staring out at the street. Her sad little face transformed when she caught sight of him sitting astride Jack.

He could hear her through the thin panes of glass, screaming with excitement for her mother to come look. A moment later, Sarah's concerned face appeared behind Becca looking to see what caused such a response from her daughter.

Quinn knew the minute Sarah realized it was he who sat on the tall gray horse outside her window. Her jaw clamped shut and her eyes sparked. It was obvious to a blind man she was still seething. But then her eyes met his. He could see sadness there and the quiver of her chin spoke volumes.

The moment he leaned forward to dismount, she closed the curtains against him and returned him to his lonely side of the world. He stuck his foot back in the stirrup and repositioned himself in the saddle. Resigned to leave her be for the moment, he pulled the reins against Jack's neck.

"Come on, Jack. Let's get outta here."

CHAPTER 12

*S*arah couldn't believe her eyes when Becca called her to the window. Quinn was sitting astride a beautiful horse looking every bit the handsome lawman he was. As much as it pained her to admit, she was very attracted to this new husband of hers.

Quinn. She wished things could be different between them, but the unbidden image of Quinn's indiscretions with Flora Lawrence just down the street from where his wife was supposed to be sleeping, was unbearable. She didn't want to be the ambivalent wife again and pretend she didn't know what was going on under her nose. She knew.

Until she was convinced of Quinn's loyalty to her, she would keep him at arm's length. It was her only armor against her attraction to the unfaithful scoundrel.

She closed the window curtains in his face hoping to dissuade him from trying to convince her otherwise. She needed time to think.

"Momma, I want to ride the horse. Why can't I ride Mr. Quinn's horse?" Becca demanded to know. Sarah knew it was only a matter of time before Becca wore Quinn down to let her ride that beast now that she knew it existed. The best she could hope for was to postpone the inevitable.

"Because it's much too big for you. And dangerous. I don't want to hear another word about it, do you understand? Now, if you want your own bedroom to sleep in by this evening, I suggest you get busy. I want to see the dust fly from under that rag."

"Yes, Mother." That was the first time Becca hadn't screamed at her when she didn't get her way since they left Charleston. Could Sarah consider it a first step in her daughter's re-acclimation to discipline, or was her daughter as tired of adversity as she was? Only the passage of time would tell. For now, she should get back to the task at hand.

Sarah had often seen the house managers of her parent's estate direct the staff of housekeepers through the mansion. She hated to admit she hadn't paid them much attention at the time. If memory served her, they covered their hair in bonnets and armed themselves with feather dusters, mop buckets and brooms. She could do this.

Sarah was just thinking about how she needed to talk with Charity, but she couldn't very well enter the saloon with Becca by the hand. Then a knock on the door signaled her first visitor since moving to Montana. She sent Becca a puzzled look. "Who could that be?"

Becca ran to the window and looked out. "It's Auntie Charity." Her daughter ran to the door and opened it wide.

Sarah followed her daughter, wondering if she'd somehow conjured her friend merely by wishing for her presence. "Come in. Come in." She welcomed Charity inside and put another log on the fire. "Let me grab a chair from the kitchen." She pulled a chair alongside the only rocking chair in the front room and offered her friend a seat. "Please, sit. What brings you by this morning? Is everything alright?"

Charity hesitated and cut a side glance toward Becca.

Sarah caught the meaning. "Becca, darling. Why don't you go find your storybooks from my trunk in the bedroom and read for a spell this morning so Aunt Charity and I can have a grownup talk."

Sarah watched her reluctant daughter do as she was asked. When the bedroom door closed behind her, Charity turned to her.

"I need to talk to you."

Sarah nodded in agreement. "Good, because I need to talk to you too."

Sarah and Charity wasted no time sharing their concerns with each other. When Charity left to go back to her husband and the saloon, Sarah was both troubled and relieved. She and her friend had similar problems. Both had fallen for their handsome husbands in the span of only a few days, and yet neither of them was convinced their husbands were honorable men. They'd decided to take a wait-and-see attitude. What other choice did they have?

Sarah and Becca worked through the rest of the afternoon, dusting, sweeping, and mopping. Once the cleaning was done, Sarah hung a heavy curtain over the small room Quinn kept his extra things in. There wasn't much in there, so it didn't take long to remove the items. Some old clothes, an unloaded shotgun. A small wooden trunk.

"What's in that, Momma?" Becca asked, pointing to the trunk. Sarah wondered much the same thing herself, but she would respect her husband's privacy.

"I don't know, Becca. It belongs to Quinn. It isn't nice to snoop in other people's things. We must wait for him to share it with us."

She could see Becca eye the trunk with curious intent. "When will that be?" Becca asked.

"I don't know, sweetheart. When he trusts us to know what's inside, I suppose."

"When will that be—"

"Becca. Enough," Sarah said with an edge to her voice. "There is much to be done." She redirected her daughter's curiosity. "Let's get your new rug into your bedroom, shall we?"

Sarah pulled the bulky rolled up rug from the main room where the mercantile owner left it along with all her other purchases. She didn't feel quite so guilty about all of Quinn's money she had spent when thoughts of his mistress came to mind.

She pushed the unpleasant thoughts aside and dragged the braided brightly colored carpet through the kitchen, moving chairs and the kitchen table to make room, and into the small former storage room off the kitchen. The rug was a perfect fit. There wasn't a single square inch of the rough board floor in the tiny room that wasn't covered by the soft wool rug.

Becca clapped her hands in delight. "It's beautiful, Momma." Becca lay on the rug and rolled around for a bit. "Where's my bed? Do I get my own bed?"

"Yes, the bed rails are in the front parlor. We will have to carry them in here and then put them together. Do you think we can do that, just you and me?"

"Of course." Becca ran from the room and Sarah followed. She laughed at the sight of her little girl's happy face. It was a blessing for certain and had been such a long time coming.

"Let's pull together, shall we?" Sarah pulled the two long boards through the little house and into Becca's new bedroom. There was just enough room for the boards to fit at the back of the room near the window.

They returned for the two short boards making the head and foot of the bed. Everything was notched and fit together like a puzzle. Next, Sarah carried the rope netting that held the mattress to the frame. Iron nails were already in the board at the right locations, so Sarah hooked the rope loops on the nails. Within minutes, the rope grid was in place. All that was left was the mattress.

The linen covered mattress was quite impressive. And heavy. Sarah pulled and tugged and pushed until she was able to get it through all the doors and into the little room. Finally, after hours of backbreaking work, Becca's room was done. Becca's small traveling trunk was emptied of her daughter's things.

Four hooks on the wall held Becca's dresses. The small chest in the corner organized stockings, camisoles, petticoats and nightgowns. There was a three-shelf bookcase next to the bed for all of Becca's books and toys and things she cherished. Sarah had to admit, everything looked amazing. It was her hard work that created this haven for Becca and she felt the pride of accomplishment. It was a good feeling.

The clock in the front parlor struck four-thirty. It would be time for Quinn to come home soon. What excuse was she going to use this time to explain why there was no supper on the stove? She heard a horse whinny from the street. She rushed to the window just in time to see Quinn ride by on his way to the stables.

Panic rushed through Sarah's heart. Perhaps if she were asleep—or maybe she could—what? Visit Charity in the saloon? "Oh, this is ridiculous." She wasn't a devious person and she couldn't keep up this charade forever. Eventually, Quinn was going to discover her lies. She might as well admit it and see where the truth would lead. She would tell him the minute he walked through that door. What was the worst that could happen? Her heart didn't want to know.

Quinn was bone tired and he was ready for a warm bath,

some warm food and a warm, willing—he pushed that thought right out of his head. He refused to force his bride into something she wasn't ready for. After all, although he was her legal husband, he was still a stranger.

He saw the heat in Sarah's eyes when she looked at him. She wanted him as much as he wanted her. So, what was holding her back? He wished he knew. After this morning's— whatever it was, he doubted she would even want him in the same house, but they needed to talk and talk they would as soon as he stabled Jack and checked on his prisoner.

Quinn had asked a couple of men in town to peek in on the prisoner from time to time throughout the day while he rode out to Matt Bailey's place. He hadn't seen any strangers in town, but he wasn't about to take any chances either by leaving his prisoner unguarded.

The ride out to Matt Bailey's place was short and uneventful. His jurisdiction extended beyond the borders of town. There was no other law enforcement, so he checked on the outlying ranches from time to time to make certain people were doin' alright.

Matt, and his new bride, Julia, lived about two miles out of town on the road that ran alongside the creek the town was named after. It was an easy thirty-minute ride and the day was glorious. The sun shone bright and warm against the sparkles of the snow, illuminating the landscape into a story-book setting for Christmas.

Quinn knew Matt's new wife was a friend of Sarah's and he'd hoped to have the opportunity to ask her about Sarah's past, but when he arrived, Matt was busy trying to herd cows into his split rail corral by himself and those cantankerous beasts didn't want to cooperate.

By the time he and Matt managed to gather them up and push them through the wild terrain of steep rock embank-ments, tall pine trees and frozen snow drifts, it was getting late and he needed to get back to town to check on his prisoner. And his unhappy wife.

Besides, traveling alone in these wild mountains at night wasn't something he wanted to chance. Signs of a roaming wolf pack were all over Matt's land and even for a seasoned soldier and a tough old war horse, it was too dangerous to be caught out after dark.

He had hoped to check on two more ranches past Matt's just to get some miles under the saddle for ole' Jack. But gathering cattle had been an all-afternoon chore and if he could count the miles he and Jack rode back and forth and up and down the mountain, he probably rode at least twenty miles or more.

The sun was low in the sky when he loped into town. He could see the glimmer of a lantern through the windows of his house when he passed. His stomach growled. He hoped Sarah had something on the stove. He hated to impose on Mrs. Lawrence again even if she was agreeable with the arrangement.

Quinn pulled Jack to a walk and guided the big gray gelding into the double open doors of the stable. Willie was there to greet him when he stepped out of his stirrups. "Hello, Sheriff. Have a nice ride?"

"Sure did, Willie. It was long overdue." Quinn straightened and stretched his leg muscles. Willie reached for the reins, but Quinn shook his head. "No, Willie. Me and Jack have been through a lot. I'll take care of him. But thanks, anyway."

Willie nodded and went back to work. Quinn lead Jack to his stall and stripped him of his saddle, blanket and bridle and hung them on the racks on the wall. The big horse shook his body and dipped his nose into the water bucket while Quinn brushed his sweaty back, the dirt and mud from his legs, and tamed his windblown midnight-colored mane and tail.

Quinn finished Jack's grooming and pulled the feed and water buckets off the hooks in the wall. After a good cleaning, he refilled them with fresh cold water and two scoops of grain. Quinn closed and latched the gate to Jack's stall and pulled a flake from the hay bin and threw it over the stall wall into the hay rack. He rubbed Jack's ears as the horse munched his dinner. "Thanks, ole boy. It was a good day, wasn't it?"

The horse bobbed his head up and down. Whether it was Quinn's fingers scratching an itch or he was just agreeing with Quinn's words, it didn't really matter. It had been a good day. He just hoped the evening would go as well.

It was getting close to four o'clock. Eugene would be coming on duty soon. In the meantime, Quinn had some work to do at the jail before he headed home. A few quick strides and he was standing in front of his office, unlocking the door. He stepped inside and listened for any unusual sounds. There were no sounds at all. He stoked the fire inside the cast iron potbellied stove. Satisfied the fire would catch, he called out to his prisoner. "Bishop? You still in there?" He had intended his question as a joke but when his prisoner didn't answer, he grew concerned.

"Bishop?" Quinn stepped inside the jail cell room, his hand on his gun just to be cautious. He peered between the bars and saw his prisoner lying on the bed. "Bishop?" The man didn't stir. Quinn's senses were now on full alert. Was there something wrong with the man or was this a trick? "Bishop!" He called out again. The man never moved.

Quinn pulled the key out of his pant pocket and unlocked the door, his gun drawn. He stepped inside the cell and poked the man's foot with the barrel of his gun. Still nothing. He couldn't tell if the man was breathing or not.

He stepped closer to the cot and reached to pull the

blanket away from the man's body. The minute he grabbed hold of the blanket, Bishop sprang to life, kicking Quinn in the gut.

Stunned and off balance, Quinn fell back against the cell's other wall. Bishop jumped on him and tried to wrestle his gun from his hand. Quinn's instincts kicked in and he punched Bishop in the face with his left hand still holding tight to his Colt revolver in his right. Bishop doubled over and tried to make it to the open cell door. Quinn was quicker. He punched the barrel of his revolver into Bishop's retreating back. "Hold it right there, you lowlife, or you'll be dead before you clear that door."

His prisoner froze in mid-stride, his hands raised above his head in surrender. "Gotta hand it to you, lawman. You is quicker than most. Last jail I broke outta, I was five miles out of town before that deputy woke up from the jail house floor."

Quinn wanted to pummel the guy, but he knew his duty. "I'm surprised you left him in good enough condition to get up off the floor. Now, get back on that bed, before I'm tempted to perform a little territory justice of my own."

His prisoner backed into the cell and sat on the bed. Quinn handcuffed the man to the iron ring in the wall. "Hey, now, you ain't gonna leave me like this, are ya? How's a man to eat? Or sleep?" Bishop whined.

"You should have thought about that before you jumped me, Bishop. Now shut up before I change my mind about letting you go so I can shoot you while trying to escape."

"Ah, that ain't right, Sheriff. That ain't right at all."

Quinn slammed the door between the cells and his office. He was still agitated when Eugene showed up for work a little early.

"What's got you all in a tizzy, Sheriff? You look like a mad hornet stuck in a milk bottle."

"Bishop tried to break out of jail. Watch the little weasel tonight. Don't trust one word that snake utters, you understand me, Deputy?" Quinn snapped his words.

"Yes, sir, Sheriff. I won't even open the man's cell door. If his food won't fit through the bars, then he ain't eatin'. Serve 'im right."

"Good. Now, I'm goin' to check around to see if any strangers are in town that might be friends of Johnny. Keep all the doors locked. I don't know if he's got buddies, but I've got a bad itch he's up to something." Quinn grabbed his hat and headed out. He waited outside his office door until he heard Eugene bolt the lock in place.

He walked around the side of the jail and checked the door between the alley and the apothecary. Locked. Good. He felt some reassurance that anyone trying to help the prisoner will have to go through one of two doors. He felt Eugene knew the danger and was prepared. As a precaution, he would come back around before bedtime and check just to be sure. He had that prickly feeling at the base of his neck he often got during the war when danger was near. And he had that feeling now.

Quinn made a quick pass toward the saloon, stepping through the doors and looking around the room for any strangers in town. Lewis stepped up behind the bar and greeted him. "Good evening, Quinn. Are you here for an evening nightcap?"

"No, Lewis. I'm on official business. Seen any strangers that might have come in today?" Quinn tried to keep his tone even and nonchalant. He didn't know anything and didn't want to stir up hysteria among the citizens.

Lewis frowned and looked around the room. "No, it's been rather slow today. Nothing out of the ordinary that comes to mind. I mean, I get people in and outta here all day and night, but nobody I'd consider a stranger. Expecting trouble?"

Quinn couldn't really say where this feeling was coming from, but he had learned long ago to trust it. "I'm a lawman. I'm always expecting trouble." He glanced around the room and nodded to some of the patrons of Lewis's saloon. "Well, if you do notice anything out of the ordinary, will you let me know?"

"Sure will, Quinn. You can count on it."

It had been a long day and he was dog tired. He checked on Eugene and the prisoner once more. Both were tight and snug for the night behind the heavy wood and iron bar doors of his office. He could relax now. It was a little after eight o'clock when Quinn finally headed home.

Sarah lay down next to Becca and read her a story. Her little girl was so tired from all the work they had done, she fell asleep before the second page. The gentle sound of Becca's soft snores made Sarah smile. She and her daughter had only spent three nights in this little house and already it was feeling more and more like home every day that passed.

She covered Becca with a quilt and rose to survey Becca's little room again. A seed of pride grew in her chest. *She* had done this. She and Becca. Not a bevy of servants who did as she told them. She had transformed this little storage room into a cute cozy nook for her daughter. It was even more beautiful than any of Becca's fancy things back in Charleston. And it was all because she had made a home for her daughter—without her in-laws or their interference.

She heard the clock strike eight o'clock. Sadness crept into Sarah's chest. Quinn wasn't home yet. She had seen him ride by several hours ago. What could be keeping him? She tried not to let her mind wander to the house down the street and its occupant. Was he refusing to come home as punishment for her outspoken comment this morning? That's how William behaved. Would Quinn?

Sarah dimmed the oil lamp sitting on the kitchen table with a heavy heart. She hated this situation between her and Quinn. She wanted her handsome husband to be just that— her husband in every sense of the word, but she didn't want to share him.

She had no right to make demands of Quinn to respect their marriage when she still harbored secrets of her own that could destroy them at any moment. And yet, in her heart, she knew she couldn't share him with the Widow Lawrence.

She planned to tell him everything tonight but she had expected him hours ago. What if he didn't come home? Perhaps she should go look for him. No, that would look like a desperate woman who couldn't hold on to her husband. As close to the truth as it was, her pride refused to allow her to play the part of a victim. Not again.

Perhaps a warm bath would do the trick and help her sleep. Quinn said there was a bath tub hanging on the back of the house. She could get it and heat water on the stove. That much she knew she could do.

The tub was hanging on a spike on the back of the house. Sarah stepped calf deep into the snow to reach it. Its icy temperature created shivers of goosebumps. She managed to lift the tub from its resting place and drag it into the house. She was surprised all the noise she made hadn't woken Becca. If her little girl was as tired as she was, it was no wonder she slept through the noise.

She placed the tub in the middle of the kitchen floor next to the table, then filled every kettle and pot she could find with water. Stoking the kitchen stove with sticks of firewood, she lit them and stood back waiting for them to catch fire.

Soon, the fire burned hot and the water began to boil. She had no idea how much work it took to take a bath. This knowledge gave her a new appreciation for her staff back home. How many times had she flicked her wrist and demanded a hot bath? She hated to think about it now.

Had her staff hated her and others like her? She hoped not, but why would they not? If she could apologize to them now for being a spoiled daughter and wife, she most certainly would.

She was careful to lift the boiling pots of water and pour them into the tub. Finally, all the pots were emptied, and she filled a bucket with cold water to temper the water enough so as not to burn her skin.

Thank goodness, Cassie Weston had the foresight to include a scented bar of bath soap in her order. Sarah placed the bar to her nose and pulled in a deep breath. *Lavender. Ahhhhhh.*

Sarah pinned her hair on top of her head and tossed a washing cloth and the scented soap into the steaming water. The kitchen was warm from the heat of the stove and there was nothing left to do but get in. What if Quinn came home while she was bathing? Her chin rose up in stubborn determination. *So, what if he did?*

With deliberate movements, she discarded her filthy clothes and piled them beside the tub. Naked and exposed, she stepped into the tub and sank deep under the hot, soapy water. Sarah was filled with amazement at the sensations sluicing over her body. She had had baths before. And yet, this was the first one she enjoyed because of her own efforts. It was exhilarating.

She had made this happen with her own two hands. This was something she knew little about, but she wanted more of it. A lot more. She wanted to be more than a pampered woman who had little regard for the efforts of others.

A sigh escaped her lips and she leaned her head back against the tub's rim. The tub wasn't long enough to support the entire length of her body, so she bent her knees and lay back in the comforting warmth of the scented water.

Sarah didn't know how long she lay there. She thought perhaps she had drifted off to sleep but for how long she hadn't a clue. The first conscious thought that popped into her mind was the whereabouts of her husband. How late was it? Where was he? Who was he with?

A slow awareness sent shivers through her body. The water had grown tepid, but it wasn't the temperature of the water that made her tremble. She sensed she was no longer alone.

She opened her eyes and collided with Quinn's. His gaze was dark and stormy, like the winter sky just before the storm set in the day she arrived. Her breath stalled in her chest and she was very much aware of her husband's masculine presence.

"Quinn." She was at a loss for words. She wasn't brave enough to say everything she wanted to say. She couldn't bring herself to ask him where he'd been. She was just glad he had come home—to her. She felt the tears sting her lids and she was afraid to speak for fear of giving her emotions away and that would mean he would hold all the power.

"Sarah." He whispered her name with reverence. "I'm sorry I'm so late. I had planned on being home much earlier but when I got back to the jail, that damned Bishop attacked me and—"

"Are you hurt?" She sat up then caught herself. She slipped back beneath the water and gathered random floating bubbles of soap to cover her nakedness.

His eyes followed her movement for a moment until they

stopped at the place where her hands disappeared under the soap screen. He was silent so long, she thought he had forgotten her question.

It was only when his attention returned to her face, that he spoke again. "No, I'm fine. Bishop isn't as smart as he thinks he is. I was prepared for his shenanigans. Federal marshal told me he would try to escape."

Sarah was relieved his delay in getting home was because of his job and not the woman down the street, although the thought of her husband hurt made her sick to her stomach.

Quinn removed his hat and coat, his eyes never leaving her. "I'm sorry I'm late. I guess that's part of being a lawman —never knowing what the day will bring. Expect the unexpected."

Sarah yearned for a connection with Quinn. "And part of being a lawman's wife, I suppose?" she asked sinking deeper into the tepid water. "Like whether or not your husband will come home at the end of the day?" Her thoughts turned to Flora Lawrence when she uttered her words. Quinn mistook her meaning.

"I guess I never thought of it that way. I've never really had anyone else to worry about except myself, Sarah. Not in a long time."

She nodded her understanding, but she didn't understand. Not at all. He seemed so sincere when he was with her. She wanted to trust him. She truly did, but she knew where he went late at night when he wasn't at home in their bed.

"I'll do a better job of keeping my wife informed of my whereabouts so you won't worry unnecessarily."

"I'd like that. If you could keep me informed, that is." She wished she had the courage to just ask him about Flora Lawrence and what the woman meant to him. She didn't. Not yet.

"Sarah, would you have any reservations about me asking

the Widow Lawrence to keep an eye on Becca tonight? I was hoping you and I could have a talk about what happened this morning. Where is Becca anyway? Asleep?"

Sarah's affection for Quinn wavered at the mention of his mistress. "You asked that woman to watch my daughter? How could you do that?"

Quinn's genuine puzzlement irked her even more. Did the man not have a clue what his affair was doing to their marriage?

"What have you got against Flora Lawrence? She's a fine woman. Hard-working. Always going out of her way to help people."

Sarah couldn't hold her tongue any longer. "Oh, yes. She's great at helping people. I wonder how many other husbands she's helped herself to." Sarah's voice cracked with emotion and she grabbed her drying towel to hide her nakedness. She felt too exposed, too vulnerable sitting in the tub.

"Helping herself to husbands? What the hell are you talking about? Flora isn't interested in another husband. She just lost hers this summer and she's still grieving for him."

Quinn's words punched a hole in Sarah's inflated anger. Worse, his indignation was unmistakable. Had she misjudged her husband? And the widow? Oh, dear God. Had William's betrayal tainted her ability to see the truth in other people?

"Sarah, is that what this is about? You think me and Mrs. Lawrence are—you think I would betray our marriage vows?" The wounded look on Quinn's face pierced her doubt completely. "Why would I do that? If I were interested in Flora, don't you think I would have married her instead of sending for a bride from Charleston, of all places?" Her heart stalled as the realization of Quinn's words hit home.

Quinn stood in front of her, hands on hips, demanding answers to his questions. The same questions she had asked herself since she saw her husband that first night at Flora

Lawrence's door. The problem was her conclusions were all wrong.

"I-I'm sorry Quinn. When I saw you sneaking down the street toward Flora's house—" she offered in explanation.

"Sneaking? Is that what you saw, Sarah?" Quinn demanded. His anger was palpable.

"That's not the word I meant to use." Her shoulders drooped in resignation. "That's not true. At the time, I did think you were sneaking down to Flora's house. I mean, I saw you walking down the dark street and then you knocked on her door when you told me you were going to work. And —she invited you inside. I didn't know you had an arrangement with her or that she was still mourning her husband. I didn't know—"

Quinn turned away from her. She had lost him.

"Please, Quinn. Give me a chance to explain." She pleaded and stood to follow him. The towel around her wet body did nothing to her shivers. It wasn't the cold from the cooling fire that made her shiver. It was the possibility her suspicions had turned Quinn against her.

He turned back toward her and froze in his tracks. He acted as if he had been hit over the head with a poleaxe. Dear God, he was so angry with her, he couldn't speak. Could she convince him to give her a chance to explain?

His eyes once again searched her face. "Sarah, please tell me what I have done to make you distrust me. What was it that caused you to think I would betray our marriage vows three days after I promised to love, honor and protect you and our daughter? Tell me, Sarah. Tell me what it was." Quinn pleaded.

She had to answer him honestly. "It wasn't you, Quinn. I know that now. I'm not a victim of your actions. I'm a victim of—my own foolishness. It was my bruised and battered ego that tried and convicted you a philanderer. Nothing you have done is responsible. I swear. It is my own tainted view of the world courtesy of my past that made me jump to the worst possible conclusion."

Her instincts told her all along his actions were at odds with her suspicions. She should have listened to her heart. Was it too late to make amends, considering she was still pretending to be something she was not?

Quinn was standing in front of her now, his strong fingers gripped her wet, bare shoulders. The look in his eyes confirmed what she must have known all along. This honest and good man would never betray her. But would he still want her when he learned the truth? The whole truth? Did she have the courage to find out?

Quinn thought he couldn't be more surprised when he walked into the kitchen and found his very naked wife asleep in a bath full of fragrant bubbles. And yet, when she accused him of having an affair with Flora Lawrence he almost laughed—until he realized she was serious.

He turned away to give himself a chance to recover from the accusation of infidelity as well as the sight of the beautiful woman up to her neck in bubbles. He thought himself in control until she rose from the tub like a goddess from the sea and stood before him in all her naked glory with nothing separating them but a water-soaked drying towel.

Water sluiced from her body evoking ripples of desire south of his gun belt.

He had known this wife of his was a beauty, but he had no idea what charms she hid beneath those many layers of winter clothing. And he couldn't be more delighted to find out.

"Sarah," he whispered. He was rooted in place and could

seem to do nothing but stare. The goosebumps covering her skin and the pucker of her nipples jutting out at him through the thin towel finally sunk into his lust-filled brain. "You must be freezing. Let's get you warmed up."

He could have wrapped her in a blanket and stoked the fire in the stove. But the fires she stoked in his blood at seeing her naked beauty prevented his brain from making that decision. All he could think of to wrap around her was him.

He pulled her into his arms. He was very much aware of her trembling body as he wrapped her in his warmth. He buried his face in her damp hair. "I want you to know without a shadow of a doubt, Flora and I have nothing between us but a contract. She provides three square meals for me and my prisoner and I pay her a fee. That's it. Nothing more. I swear on my parents' and my two brothers' graves, I would never betray our vows."

Quinn's heart beat wildly in his chest. He wondered where her distrust came from. Flora's words came back to remind him. He needed to learn what had happened in her previous life to think the worst of him.

He wrapped her towel around her body and picked her up in his arms. The urge to kiss her nearly sent him to his knees but he knew if he did, he would never get to the talking part and they had a lot to discuss.

He navigated around the kitchen table and turned to fit them through the kitchen door. He was almost to the bedroom with his naked wife, when he realized there was another woman in his life unaccounted for. "Where's Becca sleeping?" he whispered close to Sarah's ear. It was more of a gesture he couldn't resist than fear of being overheard.

"She's in her own bed sleeping. She and I finished her room today. It looks lovely—" Quinn silenced his wife's lips with the kiss he had been wanting to give her since the moment he walked in that back door.

Oh, it wasn't that he didn't want to hear all about her hard work. He did—just not right now. Right now, he had other pressing matters on his mind. And in his jeans.

He didn't release Sarah's lips until he knelt on the bed and gently lay her among the bedsheets. The look she gave him nearly melted his soul.

Quinn took a deep breath to calm his runaway heart and slow his passion. And yet, he never took his eyes off Sarah's. He couldn't. Her desire held him spellbound, and it nearly unmanned him. But, he wanted this moment, the first time they pledged their bodies to each other as husband and wife, to be a special moment shared only by the two of them. And he wasn't certain they could do that until they chased away their ghosts from their pasts.

Quinn dropped his gun belt to the floor and closed the bedroom door to give them the privacy they needed. There was a lot at stake between them and it was time for them both to discover each other's secrets.

CHAPTER 13

*S*arah slipped beneath the sheets and waited for her husband to join her, but she was disappointed.

He turned from the locked door and pulled up the chair next to the bed. She watched him take a deep breath.

"Quinn? I thought you were—we were going to—" she stammered, unsure what to say to the man sitting beside her bed. Why wasn't he *in* her bed?

The heated look in his amber-colored eyes sent ripples of desire through her core. She had never wanted a man so much and yet there he sat, in a chair, by the side of her bed. What was she to think about his behavior?

"Sarah." He whispered her name with reverence. She held her breath, waiting for what would come next. Was this how he would set her free? Is that what was happening between them? He was looking for the words to tell her he didn't want her as his wife and their marriage was a mistake?

"Sarah, I assure you I want nothing more than to join you in that bed and make you my wife in every sense of the word."

Her panic slowed at his words. "Then why are you sitting in the chair and not—"

"Because we won't say the things that need to be said before we fall into each other's arms. I think we both know— there are things we need to tell each other before we go any further, don't you?"

Adrenalin pulsated through her body catching her breath and holding it hostage. *He knew.* He was a lawman. How did she think she could hide being wanted by the law from a lawman? He was giving her a chance to explain. She needed to tell him everything if she had any hope he would help her.

She nodded in agreement and sat up in bed, resting against her pillow. Nervous fingers pulled at the bedcovers to hide her nakedness. *Courage, Sarah. You can do this.*

"Very well, Quinn." Sarah's joy faded when she realized she and Quinn couldn't move forward until she was honest with him. She owed him the truth. All of it. Heat burned in his eyes when he looked at her and scorched her to her core. Would his eyes still hold that same desire for her when he learned of her deceit?

She was at a loss as to how to proceed so she stalled. "What would you like to talk about? You know, Christmas is only six weeks away. Should I be dropping hints for Santa?" she teased, hoping to dispel the tension building in her chest.

He looked at her for a second longer as if weighing a decision in his mind. Then, he said. "Why don't we start with William."

Sarah was caught completely off guard. "Why would you want to know about William? He's…dead."

"Yes, I know that much. Otherwise, you wouldn't be here —in my bed—now would you?"

She knew he was teasing her back, but she didn't want to think about William. Or Charleston. She wanted her previous life to just go away and leave her be.

"What do you want to know about William that you don't already know? He was in the Confederate Army and he was killed. End of a very sad story."

"How long was he a soldier?"

Sarah hesitated. "Only a few months."

"A few months? But that was at the very end of the war. Why would he join so late? That—doesn't make sense. The war was lost by then. Why risk his life for a lost cause?" Quinn pushed for answers she didn't want to give him. "Sarah, what are you not telling me?" He turned to face her.

"William's father insisted he go. He said it would be an embarrassment to the family if he didn't do his duty. I begged William not to go. But, he refused to listen—to his wife."

William's father's words echoed cruelly in her ears. *"It's your fault he's dead because you failed in your duty as my son's wife. You badgered him with your selfish words and accusations of abandonment that made him doubt his decision to go. And it was that doubt that put him in harm's way."*

Quinn reached out across the bed and wiped away a tear she hadn't known she'd shed. "What is it, Sarah? I sense something is eating away at you. Tell me what it is. Please."

Sarah knew she should tell Quinn everything. He was a good man. A dependable man. But could she trust him to be a loyal man? Would he choose her if it came down to her and the law?

"Sarah? I can see little gears grinding between those pretty little ears of yours. Tell me what's troubling you." Quinn's insistence pushed her a little closer to trusting him. She hoped she wasn't making a mistake.

"Quinn," She inhaled a deep breath for courage. "There are some things you need to know about my life in Charleston—and some things you are going to wish you didn't.

"I should have told you everything the day we were

married. I should have pulled you aside in that church and explained why I escaped Charleston with only my daughter and my friends."

She raised her gaze to her husband's, took a deep breath, and pushed onward.

"My husband was killed at the end of the war. You already know that."

"Tell me what he was like."

He watched her. Finally, he said. "You can trust me with your secrets, Sarah. All of them."

Her shoulders slumped in resignation. The ghost of a wistful smile smoothed her lips, curling them up at the corners. "I'm not certain talking about the past will help either one of us, but if you must know—"

"I do. It will help me understand how to be a better husband, don't you think so?"

Sarah nodded in agreement. She took a deep breath and began. "William was so handsome. He was the catch of Charleston, or so everyone said. Perhaps that is why I wanted him so much.

"William and I were introduced and hit it off immediately. We were the talk of the town. We married and set up residence in a beautiful townhouse on a tree shaded avenue. It was the idyllic life. Until Becca was born."

"Why would Becca's birth cause problems? She's a lovely little girl."

Sarah's brows rose in question.

"Yes, even when she's not exactly acting lady-like, she's still a beautiful child." Quinn offered in explanation.

Sarah smiled at his comment. He was so kind and gentle with Becca. She continued.

"William wasn't much for the domestic lifestyle after all. He liked to gamble and race his horses all over the countryside. And, as it turns out, he had an eye for beautiful women."

Quinn remained quiet. She wondered what he was thinking but another part of her didn't want to know. In for a penny, in for a pound—

"I was naïve and William was selfish. He took advantage of my confinement and wandered off the marriage path. When I found out about it, he dismissed my heartache as silly and kept on about his business."

Now maybe Quinn could understood where her suspicions about him and Flora had come from. Not from something he had done, but from something William had done.

"There's more. My in-laws are very ambitious, cruel people. They had little esteem for their son. They had less regard for his widow."

Quinn remained silent.

"The short version of this nightmare is my daughter is the Caldwells only heir now, with William dead. They wanted to control her and to do that, they had to control me. When I refused to play their games, they hired witnesses to swear lies about me. Then, they bought a judge and jury who declared me unfit to raise my own daughter."

Her voice cracked with emotion, but Quinn never moved. Her confidence waivered.

"Go on, Sarah. Tell me all of it. I need to know the rest."

Nervous chills had her seeking more bedcovers to warm her naked body. She stumbled over her emotions wishing Quinn would join her beneath the covers. His refusal put fear into her already quivering heart.

"I—refused to give up my daughter without a fight. So, with no money, no home and no hope against William's wealthy and well-connected parents, my friends and I answered the advertisement for brides wanted in Montana Territory.

"And once I had an escape plan, I sneaked into their house under cover of darkness—and stole my daughter back. My friends and I boarded a steamboat the next morning and here we are."

She studied her husband who was looking at her as if seeing her for the first time. She couldn't stand it. She had to know what he was thinking.

"What are you thinking, Quinn?"

He took a few minutes to answer. "You used my proposal of marriage as the means to kidnap your daughter back from your in-laws, is that what you are telling me?" His expression reflected the shock in his voice.

Unsure what to say, she remained quiet and waited to hear what her lawman husband would say next.

"Sarah." He whispered her name and closed his eyes. "What have you done?"

Resigned to the fact her short marriage was about to end, she raised her chin in defiance and met her husband's troubled gaze. "I did what any mother would do for her child, and I would do it all over again to save my daughter. I'm sorry if you feel I used you, Quinn. I had no choice. Those people left me no other choice."

Her voice cracked with emotion. Regret settled bitter in her stomach. She knew the truth now. Quinn was a lawman at heart. She couldn't count on him any more than she had been able to count on William. Her prayers were not to be answered and her Christmas wish was not to be granted. What would happen to her and Becca now?

Quinn sat stone still in the chair and listened to his wife share her secrets. He knew she had a past full of pain and sorrow. He had no idea the extent of how much his beautiful wife and little girl had suffered because of that past.

Sarah was wanted for kidnapping her own daughter. It

was unthinkable. He needed to send a telegram to a friend of his back in New York who had the connections to find out if there was a real threat coming from Charleston. If there was an arrest warrant, he needed a plan.

As bad as Sarah's confession of being wanted had been, her story of her dead husband's infidelity relieved a lot of Quinn's suspicions after Sarah accused him of having indiscretions with Flora. But he was in utter disbelief when she told him not only had William's parents blamed her for the infidelity, they actually condoned their son's behavior.

Sarah also confided they had blamed her for William's untimely death even though they were the ones who persuaded him to join the lost cause. Then, while she was deep in grief, these same people stripped her of her home, her possessions and extorted any means of support from hers and her daughter.

Sarah's soft sobs tore at his heart. He had two choices the way he saw it. Walk away from this new family of his or dig in for the long haul and protect them from whatever came at them.

It was no wonder Sarah was so skittish and suspicious. He could only imagine the torment and confusion poor little Becca had lived through. She didn't know who to believe. Well, one thing was certain, they could both put their trust in Quinn because he would never let that little girl or her mother down. He would protect Becca and Sarah with his life. Of that fact, he would leave no room to doubt.

He looked at the beautiful woman who sat in his bed, her heart breaking and her shoulders sagging under the weight of the world. He realized then he would lay down his life for this woman without thinking twice.

He stood. Her eyes, full of fear, followed his every move. She was so beaten down by her past, she had no hope in her future. Their future. She had no faith in people who had professed to love her. Well, from this day forward, she could place her faith in him.

He unbuttoned his shirt, his gaze never wavering from his wife's beautiful face. He unbuckled his gun belt and placed it on the chair he had just vacated.

"What—are you doing?" Sarah's eyes rounded in surprise.

"I'm coming to bed. Isn't that what you wanted me to do, or did you change your mind already. Ah, what am I to do with such a fickle wife?"

He unfastened his pants and slid them down his thighs, careful to keep his eyes trained on his wife's beautiful face. She blushed as her eyes took in his nakedness.

"Sarah, I think there are some things about me you should know too. Can I join you in our marriage bed? It might be easier to tell you what I have to say if you aren't looking at me like that."

Her sultry dark eyes met his. Her love for him was plain to see. It was time they both trusted each other with the ugly truth. Life wasn't pretty sometimes, and the war had been hell on both of them.

She nodded and folded back the covers to invite him in. He slipped between the sheets, but he didn't reach for her. Not yet. He saw the uncertainty in her eyes and he knew he had to tell her now.

"Sarah, I've been keeping a secret from you too. I want you to know everything before you—before we—consummate this marriage. Nothing can be between us. Nothing at all. Agreed?"

He could tell she wasn't certain she wanted to know the truth, but he owed her the whole truth before he made her his—forever.

"Sarah?"

He watched her hesitate for another moment then exhaled a soft sigh. "Agreed."

"Good." He pulled her pillow from behind her back and put it with his own to make a soft place to lean against the bed's hard pine headboard.

"Come here. Lay next to me while I tell you another sad tale of loss and heartache."

She scooted next to him and lay in the curve of his arm. He pulled her against his side and held her close for a few moments, savoring the feel of her skin touching his. Sarah lay quiet beside him, her fingers reached up and smoothed the faded white scar across his jaw. He reached out and fingered the necklace she wore around her neck, both symbols of their past.

He took a deep breath for courage and met her beautiful soulful eyes.

"When you first learned I fought for the Union, you were angry—"

"Quinn, I told you I was sorry. I didn't mean what I said."

"I know you didn't mean it. I bring that night up because you weren't the only one with prejudices about that damned war. The truth is I chose you *because* you were a Confederate widow, not despite the fact. I chose you as my bride, so I could make some small measure of restitution to all those men in gray I killed in battle. So, you see, my dear Sarah, I used you as much as you used me. Don't you think that's a bit ironic?"

He watched the truth of his words dawn on his wife's face in the ghost of a smile gracing her lips.

"Well aren't we the pair. I suppose no one needs a bigger Christmas miracle than the two of us now that our secrets have been exposed. Where do we go from here, Quinn?"

Quinn touched the top of Sarah's head with his lips in a tender kiss and leaned back against the headboard to stare at the bedroom's ceiling. "I'm afraid there's more, Sarah."

He heard a sigh escape his wife's lips. He looked down at her to gage her reactions.

Sarah tipped her head back to look at him, her incredulous look of disbelief was almost comical. He might have laughed if he hadn't been so afraid of her reaction to what he was getting ready to tell her.

She sat up and turned to look at him, pulling the sheets to hide her nakedness. His eyes caressed her face, committing every curve to memory. That may be all he had left after—

"Just say it, Quinn. What is it you need to tell me?" Her words pleaded with him, but her eyes held dread.

He reached for her hand and used her fingers to trace the ugly scars on his side, his stomach and his upper thigh. She followed her fingers with her eyes and then searched his face for answers.

"I should have told you this the day you stepped off that stage, before we got married. I should have given you the opportunity to make the decision whether to marry me or not. I realize that now and I won't blame you one bit if you decided to leave me and never look back. I'm just hoping you won't do that—to us."

"Quinn, you are scaring me. Just say it. Whatever it is, we'll deal with it. What could be worse than learning your wife might be a fugitive from the law and on top of that, she can't cook a lick."

He inhaled a deep breath and let it out slow, his breath ruffled the hairs on top of her head.

"Sarah, I—I was injured in the war. I suffered a very serious wound. And, that injury—according to the surgeon that saved my life…" His words trailed off.

"It's okay, Quinn. Tell me what has you so troubled." Her hands roamed over his stomach and chest. He pulled her close and hugged her, kissing the top of her head, praying for a miracle.

"The surgeon said my injury was quite severe and caused trauma to my body in a way that would prevent—"

Sarah smiled at him. "I understand what you are trying to tell me and I can assure you this is something we can work on together. As a couple. A. Very. Married. Couple.

"Sarah, are you sure you truly understand—?"

"Oh, I think I do understand, Quinn. And whatever else is left to be said, can it not wait until tomorrow? I can think of other things a wife and a husband could do with their daughter is sound asleep in the next room, can't you?" His very naked wife snuggled against him and her fingers traced his stomach and disappeared under the bedcovers.

He was suddenly quite certain he believed in Christmas miracles after all.

CHAPTER 14

*S*arah awoke to dawn's gentle light peeking through the clean windows of her and her husband's bedroom. *Her husband.*

Slowly, another dawning settled soft and sweet in her conscious thoughts. She was a married woman in every sense of the word. Thoughts of the night before kicked her pulse into an undulating swell. She could still feel Quinn's touch as his tender fingers explored her body freely. He knew her worst secrets and he had chosen her. He. Chose. Her.

Sarah smiled at the thought and stretched her sore limbs. William had loved her with his body but never with his heart. Quinn loved her completely. A soft sigh passed through her smile.

"Am I to assume that is the sound of a contented woman?"

Quinn's voice interrupted her thoughts. Her first instinct was to play coy and deny she was affected at all. It was what she had done with William. She wondered now why had she done that? If she had shared her love with him more openly, would he have strayed? She couldn't be sure. Her instincts told her William was cut from a different cloth than Quinn.

"Don't be smug, dear husband." She smiled at Quinn lying in the bed next to her. "But, yes, I will admit, this is the look of a very contented woman."

Quinn turned to her, his elbow bent against his pillow, his head resting in the palm of his hand. He was watching her, and she wondered what was going through his mind when he reached out and pulled a long strand of her bed-tousled hair through his fingers, tugging her closer. He grinned at her and said. "I suppose a gentleman would apologize for last night."

Sarah's heart stuttered. "Apologize? For what?" She tried not to let her mind jump into old habits of suspicion, but her courage slipped as she waited in anticipation for what he would say next.

He wiggled his eyebrows in her direction and the intimate sensation of his fingers still twirling her hair alongside the mischievous grin stretched across his handsome face made her stomach somersault with expectation.

"I'm sorry I got home so late. And, I'm sorry it took us so long to trust each other enough to share the complications of our pasts."

She grinned at her husband and caressed his face with her lips. "Is that what we are calling it—complications?"

"For lack of a better word, I suppose. But do you know what I'm most sorry about?" He rolled her over and lay on top of her.

She relished the feel of his weight on her and she giggled. Like a silly school girl. "No, what are you most sorry about?" She could only imagine.

"I'm most sorry that we, you and me, weren't able to act like a real husband and wife last night until well after midnight. If only we could have started much sooner—"

Quinn dipped his dark head and kissed her with the passion of an experienced lover. She gladly kissed him back.

His fingers began to roam over her body and she succumbed once more to her husband's gifted hands.

Her stomach fluttered. "Quinn, I think you should write a letter to your surgeon and tell him he was mistaken." Sarah watched her husband hesitate.

He lifted his head and met her gaze. "What do you mean, the surgeon was mistaken?"

She grinned at him and nudged his manhood with her body "I think that would be obvious after last night's activities."

Confusion etched her husband's handsome face. Had she said something wrong? She thought her husband would be as happy as she was to learn he was able to perform his husbandly duties.

Quinn sat up and pulled her with him. "Sarah, I thought you said you understood what I was trying to tell you last night. What exactly do you think I was talking about last night?"

She was suddenly self-conscious of her nakedness and pulled the covers to cover herself. "I—thought you were talking about—your injuries. You said the surgeon said your injury was quite severe and caused trauma to your body in a way that would prevent you from having intimate relations with your wife." Her face pinked with embarrassment. Was Quinn really forcing her to have this conversation with him in the light of day?

Her husband pulled away from her and scrubbed his day old beard with his hands. "No, Sarah. That's not it. That's not it at all."

Her husband looked upset.

She sat up and leaned against the bed's headboard. "What is it then?"

Quinn stared at a spot on the wall as if looking for answers. After a few moments of silence, he took a deep breath and spoke, his words of regret sent shivers of fear into her tender heart.

Sarah searched his face for a sign of what he was trying so hard not to say. "Quinn, you are scaring me. Just say it. Whatever it is, we'll deal with it."

Her husband looked so sad. She took his hand in hers and pulled him to her, wrapping her arms around his waist. Her cheek against his chest, she waited. Whatever it was he had to say, she refused to let it tear them apart. Not after they had just found happiness with each other.

Quinn inhaled a deep breath and let it out slow, his breath tickled the hairs on top of her head. She remained quiet to give him a chance to gather his courage. Whatever it was, it must be something awful.

"Sarah, I told you I was injured in the war. That I suffered a very serious wound. And, that injury caused trauma to my body in a way that prevents—"

"Just say it, Quinn." Her nerves grated against her patience. She leaned back and forced his eyes to meet hers. "Whatever it is, we'll get through this."

He nodded and pulled her close again as if he couldn't bear to expose his truth without the feel of her body near. "The surgeon said it was highly unlikely that I would ever be able to—have children."

It took a full second or two for his words to register meaning inside her brain. "Are you telling me you can't give me more children? Is that your big secret, Quinn? You were injured in the war and you can't father a child?"

"That's what I'm telling you. The same cannon blast that almost killed me and my horse, Jack—left me unable to father any children. If you stay married to me, Sarah, your daughter, will be your only child.

"Look, I know I should have told you about this in my letters. I can't even explain to you why I didn't. Maybe I thought you had a child and she would be enough for both of us." He hesitated. "But I will understand if you don't want to stay married to a man who can't—"

Sarah cupped her husband's handsome face in her hands and made him look at her. She smiled and settled a gentle kiss on his lips. "Quinn, the way I see it, it's one man's word against another man's determination. I'm certain you are a very determined man when you put your mind to something. So, how about let's prove that surgeon of yours wrong, shall we?"

~

Two hours later, Quinn walked his morning rounds, checking doors, peering in windows, looking for any of the usual signs of criminal activity. But the whole time he was nodding to early morning passersby and rattling door knobs, his mind was replaying the conversation he had with his wife between the sheets early this morning. Sarah had accepted his infirmity with grace. She was such an amazing woman.

Quinn finished his rounds with the same smile he started with and he was still grinning when he stopped by the jail to relieve Eugene.

He knocked on the door and heard the office chair legs scrape against the rough floorboards. Footsteps followed, and the door opened to reveal a very haggard looking Eugene.

Quinn stepped inside and closed the door behind him. "What's going on? You look like you been rode hard and put up wet." Quinn walked to the stove to pour himself a cup of coffee. The pot was empty. He shot a curious look to his deputy.

"It was a rough night, Sheriff. That Bishop is an ornery

cuss. Hollered all night. Said he was gonna wear me down until I fell asleep then he was gonna escape."

Quinn stuck his head inside the jail cells. Bishop was sawing logs. "He's not too worried about it now. What do you think made him think he could break out? Unless he's expecting help, there's not a chance in hell he's getting outta here. I'll check again at the boarding house and the saloon to see if any strangers are staying in town."

"I think he's fulla you-know-what. But he shore was a burr under my saddle last night. I'm headin' home iffin you ain't got any objections to that, Sheriff. I'm beat."

"No, you go on. I'll have Sarah bring my breakfast here this morning. Now, off to bed. You look rough."

"I feel rough." Eugene grabbed his hat and coat from the hall tree by the front door. "I swear, Sheriff, I was about ready to plug 'im last night just to get 'im to shut up talkin'."

Quinn laughed, hoping Eugene was kidding. "Glad you didn't. The federal marshal wouldn't take too kindly to us shootin' his prisoner. Now, will you stop by my house on your way home and ask Sarah to bring breakfast here? I don't feel good about leaving knowing there might be trouble."

"Sure thing, Sheriff. I'm going right this minute."

Eugene nodded and left by the front door. Quinn checked his gun belt and ammunition. Why was Bishop all of a sudden so damn sure he was gettin' out? He couldn't escape without help. Nobody in town would help him. And there were no strangers in town. At least, none he had spotted. He would just have to keep his eyes open for trouble.

Quinn made a fresh pot of hot, black coffee and settled into his chair. It wasn't long before thoughts of Sarah and Becca leached into his thoughts. Those Caldwells musta been some kinda people to put Sarah and Becca through all that hell.

As soon as the telegraph office opened this morning, he

was gonna send a telegram to his long-time friend, John Mallory. They went way back and John had the kind of connections to find out whether Sarah's in-laws were planning on pursuing Sarah and taking Becca away from her.

Until he got word from his friend, he would watch out for his new family. And if the news wasn't good and there was a legitimate arrest warrant out for Sarah, he would just have to cross that bridge over troubled water when he came to it. He just hoped he remembered how to swim.

~

Quinn was still waiting for Sarah to bring breakfast two hours later and now Bishop was being a real pain in his ass. "Stop your yappin', Bishop. I'm gettin' your damned breakfast now."

Quinn locked the door behind him and made the short walk home in less than two minutes. He pulled off his muddy boots and, sock-footed, he stepped unannounced into his little kitchen and stood in stunned silence. It took his brain a moment to catch up with what his eyes were telling him he saw.

He must have made some sound of disbelief. It was at that very moment his new bride spun on her heels and, in wide-eyed shock, demanded to know, "What are you doing here?"

He scanned the room once more to be certain his eyes weren't playing tricks on him. Nope. The scene before him was indescribably, but painfully, real. There was flour over every square inch of the kitchen. The walls. The floor. Sarah's face. And were those eggs dripping from the ceiling? "I—came home to get my prisoner's breakfast. I told Eugene to come by and ask you to bring it, but—"

"He did come by and I'm working on it—breakfast, I mean." Sarah stammered and wrung her hands in her dirty apron. "I—I was cooking breakfast—attempting to cook breakfast, when I opened the flour sack, I dropped it and it split wide open belching flour everywhere."

He looked around again. "I see."

Becca chose that moment to run into the room, her ragged stuffed toy in her arms. "Mr. Quinn! Look! Mommy made a mess!"

Quinn glanced around the room again when an eggshell let loose its grip from the ceiling and landed smack dab in the middle of Sarah's forehead. Yellow yolk and uncooked whites ran down his wife's pretty nose. He was tempted to ask how it was possible the eggs were on the ceiling and not in the skillet but there was no time.

"Fire!" Quinn ran to the stove and covered the cast iron skillet full of hot, smoking lard with a lid to smother the erupting flames. It was then he noticed the floor in front of the stove was covered with strips of uncooked bacon.

He really wanted to ask questions about what the hell had happened to his wife—and his kitchen—during the time he had been gone, but Sarah's sobs pulled him up short.

She was a sight, covered as she was in flour and egg. She dropped into one of the kitchen chairs and pulled her dirty apron up to hide her face while she sobbed openly. He and Becca closed in on the pitiful form of his wife.

"Sarah? Um. Can I help?" He looked around the room and added, "Somehow."

"No, there's no help to be had for this mess. None at all. It's a disgrace. I'm a disgrace." Quinn thought he understood his wife's mumbling sobs, but he couldn't be certain.

"Why are you a disgrace? What happened, Sarah? It can't be that bad, now can it?" Quinn squatted next to the sobbing form of his wife to coax her into explaining the explosion of food all over the kitchen.

"Don't you have eyes, Quinn? Can't you see it is that bad and it's all my doing." Sarah hiccupped.

"Tell me what happened, Sarah. Just slow down and tell me what went wrong." He looked around the room once more, then sent a questioning look to Becca who was trying to console her mother on her other side. Her little shoulders shrugged.

"Momma was trying to cook breakfast, Mr. Quinn," Becca offered. "I don't think she can."

"I see that, Becca. I can sure enough see that."

CHAPTER 15

"*B*ecca's right, Quinn. I can't cook."

"Oh, of course you can cook, Sarah. This isn't that bad. I mean every woman has a kitchen disaster at some time or other." Quinn was trying to be kind, but she knew he didn't understand what was happening right in front of him.

"You don't understand, do you? I. Can't. Cook. Period. I was raised in a wealthy family. We had...servants."

She could tell by the look on his face he was starting to come to grips with what she was telling him by the knowing expression on his face.

"Ahhhhhh. I see." Was all the response he gave her.

Did he really see? Maybe she should explain in more detail so there was no chance her husband could misunderstood this situation.

"Quinn, we—my family—had servants to wash our clothes and cook our meals and do our biddings. Last night was the first time I have ever drawn my own bath. In my entire life, I'm embarrassed to say. I feel so—useless."

Quinn pulled up a chair at the table and sat next to her. He pulled her hands into his and made her look at him.

"Sarah. Why didn't you say something? I would have understood. "

"Before last night, I was just too afraid you wouldn't—want a flawed wife."

Quinn turned to look at Becca standing on the other side of the table studying the adults with curious intent. "Becca, honey. Isn't it time for you to get ready for school?

"It's Saturday. She doesn't have school today." Sarah explained.

Quinn nodded his understanding. "Well, that's even better because now you can run over to the Widow Lawrence's house. I bet she would give you one of those yummy cinnamon rolls she makes." He sniffed the air. "If I'm not dreamin', I think I can smell them hot out of the oven from here."

Becca's frown turned right side up at the thought of those delicious pastries.

Sarah interrupted her daughter's delightful squeal. "Quinn, she can't go alone. She's too little."

Becca's frown returned and she posted her fisted hands on her hips. "I'm not a little girl anymore, Momma. I'm six years old and I'm in the first grade now. Mrs. Schultz said I was very bright too. That means I'm really smart."

Quinn laughed at Becca's precocious, matter-of-fact declaration of her intelligence.

"Yes, you are very smart, and it's just across the street, Sarah. She'll be fine." He nodded his approval to Becca. "Now, go get your coat and mittens and scarf. I want to see you before you leave to make certain you are bundled up all nice and toasty, okay Becca?"

"Sure, Quinn. I'll be right back." Becca ran from the kitchen to her little room. Sarah heard rustling and drawers slammed shut. There was even a loud crash of some sort. "It's alright, I knocked my storybooks off the bookshelf." Becca's voice called out from her room.

Quinn grinned at Sarah. Her sobs now diminished to unladylike hiccups. She grinned back.

Becca was back in moments and Sarah watched her handsome husband interact with her daughter. It touched her in a way no other person had ever done.

Quinn's deep laughter sent shivers up her spine. He laughed at Becca because she had buttoned her coat crooked, the right side was four inches longer than the left. Her scarf was wound around her neck all the way up to her nose and her stocking hat was pulled down so low he couldn't see her eyes. She was a mess, just like her mother, a pampered princess, but Quinn praised her efforts anyway.

"Good job, Becca. Look at you, all grown up. Would you mind if I make a few adjustments for you? I wouldn't want you to walk into something because you couldn't see."

She sidled up to him and allowed him access to her coat and scarf.

Quinn re-buttoned Becca's coat and re-adjusted her scarf. He held out her mittens, so she could place her thumbs in the proper holes. "There. All set." Quinn grinned in satisfaction. Sarah couldn't stem the happiness in her heart. Tears burned her eyes at the sight of Quinn's tender care of her daughter.

" Thank you, Quinn. Now can I go?" Becca's energy radiated through her beautiful blue eyes.

"Yes, now you can go, but walk straight to Widow Lawrence's house and you stay there until I or your mother come to get you, do you understand? We'll be there to get you soon."

"I will, Quinn." Sarah watched her daughter give Quinn a big hug, then she ran around the table and kissed Sarah on her flour-dusted cheek. "Bye Momma."

Sarah hugged her little girl. "Don't forget to look both

ways, Becca. Watch for horses and wagons when you cross the street."

"I will, Momma. *Now* can I go?" Becca danced in anticipation.

Sarah smiled at her daughter. "Yes, Becca. Now you can go." She watched her little dervish rush out the front door with a very un-southern-belle-like slam.

The house was now quiet with only the occasional noise from the street out front penetrating the warm and cozy little home.

Quinn turned to her. "Is there anything else we need to talk about?"

She shook her head. "No, you know everything now. Can you still love me?"

The look he gave her melted her insides. He pulled her out of her chair and into his lap, dismissing her fears of soiling his coat and pants with the leftovers of her cooking disaster.

"Oh, I think I can manage that—somehow."

CHAPTER 16

*S*arah sat in her kitchen of disaster after her husband left in search of his prisoner's breakfast. He said it was too late to expect Flora to provide for his prisoner's bottomless belly, so he headed over to Ona Jenkin's bakery next door.

The silence gave her time to think about the last day's events. Quinn's delicious kisses made her wish for nightfall, but it was his words of love vibrating deep in his chest against her cheek as he held her close that made her hope for the future a possibility.

"Sarah, there's nothing more I want to do in this world than to love you. In the morning. In the evening. At night. For the rest of our lives. I couldn't care less whether you can cook or not. I can cook. We won't starve, and in time, you will learn."

She looked up into his beautiful eyes to gauge his sincerity. She had heard words of deceit before and she guarded her heart against them, but when his gaze met hers, there was no hint of duplicity—only the look of a man in love. She had found her Christmas miracle. And yet—

She had been shocked to hear Quinn confess to her his surgeon's prediction that he would not father children. Could it really be true? Were her husband's injuries so severe, he would never give her more children? From all outward appearances, the doctor was sadly mistaken. Her husband was quite gifted in the marriage bed, but did that mean his doctor could have been wrong? Only time would tell.

Sarah roused herself from her musings and cleaned herself up. She wished she had time to visit Charity. There was so much she wanted to talk about to her friend, but she needed to offer some explanation to the Widow Lawrence as to why she sent her daughter over so early and unannounced. She donned her hooded cloak and left the house.

A few moments later, she knocked on the widow's front door and waited for her to answer. Becca answered the door almost immediately. "Hi, Momma. Come see what Miss Flora and I are making for Christmas."

Flora welcomed her into her home "Come in. Come in. I hope everything is alright this morning. I was surprised when Becca showed up at my doorstep. Delighted, mind you, but surprised. Is everything okay?"

"I'm so sorry to send her over so early and without notice. but Quinn and I, we needed some privacy, and—" Sarah stumbled over her words.

"Look, Momma. we cut out paper snowflakes and the hangers are made of lace with glass beads. See how they sparkle in the candlelight. Aren't they all so beautiful? I can't wait to show my friends at school."

Sarah forced her attention to what Becca was saying.

Becca held up one of the homemade Christmas ornaments and twirled it in her fingers, so Sarah could see it. "Yes, sweetheart. It is very beautiful. It's—beautiful." Sarah's voice cracked with emotion.

Flora frowned at Sarah. "Becca, dear, why don't you go into the kitchen and help yourself to some of those muffins I made this morning. And, pour yourself a glass of cold milk. Your momma and I will be along in a bit."

Sarah watched her daughter skip across the floor carefully holding one of her snowflake ornaments in the air and disappear into the kitchen. "Thank you, Flora. I just needed a moment to—gather my thoughts."

"Are you okay, Sarah? You seem upset. Why don't you sit down and tell me what has happened? Is it Quinn? Has he done something or said something to upset you?" Flora offered her a chair in front of the fire. Sarah accepted the woman's offer of a place to sit and her unspoken offer to listen.

"No. He's been nothing but understanding and patient. I don't exactly know where to start." Sarah offered searching her mind to make sense of the last few days.

"Start wherever you wish. Take your time. Would you like some coffee?" Flora asked.

Sarah shook her head no and met the worried look of the woman she had falsely accused of sleeping with her husband. She was embarrassed now by her suspicions. Perhaps, she should start there.

"I should probably confess to you that until last night, I thought you were sleeping with my husband."

She watched Flora sit back in her chair in shock. "What on earth would make you think that your husband and I— were—are being deceitful? Quinn and I are just friends—I swear to you, Sarah, there's nothing between Quinn and me except our business arrangement. I cook for him and his prisoners, and he pays me. I mean I'm quite fond of your husband—but not like that."

Sarah reached over and squeezed Flora's hand. "I know that now. Quinn is an honorable man and you are a kind and loving person. Of course, neither you nor my husband would dream of such behavior. My suspicions were unfounded, and my perceptions were based upon—past experiences."

Flora laughed. "Sarah, my dear girl, that's what makes us who we are. Without our past experiences, we never grow as human beings."

Sarah watched the widow pause for a moment, the sadness in her eyes reflected by the flickering flames of the fire in the fireplace.

Flora continued. "There will never be room in my heart for anyone but my Walter. He was my one true love and our time has come and gone. God rest his soul."

"I'm truly sorry I ever thought you would—" Sarah offered another heartfelt apology.

"Now, not so fast. Don't think for a minute this old woman ain't got an eye for a handsome man when she sees one. And, if I were of a mind to look for a new love—which I'm not—and, if that handsome husband of yours were single —which he isn't because he is quite smitten with his new bride and daughter—and if he were interested in a woman nearly twice his age—which he isn't, because again, he's in love with a certain beauty from Charleston—then I might have given you a run for that man's heart. As it is, you have nothing at all to worry about."

Flora's comments surprised her, but the woman's mischievous grin spoke loud and clear. The woman was teasing her. Sarah grinned back glad to have her concerns out in the open. She liked Flora Lawrence and she would treasure her as a new friend. A new friend she wanted to trust.

"There's something else, Flora. Something I find rather embarrassing to tell you."

"Well, the best way to get something off your chest is just open your mouth and say it. All at once. Like ripping off a bandage from a wound. It hurts like the dickens, but then you are done. Otherwise, it just keeps on hurtin' a little at a time."

Sarah agreed so she opened her mouth and blurted out the truth before she could talk herself out of it. "I can't cook. Not a lick. It wasn't something I was required to learn—growing up as I did." Sarah didn't add the rest of the details. She assumed Flora could read between the lines.

Flora grinned at her. "Well, I'll tell you a little secret about myself. I wasn't much of a cook either when I married Walter. There are so many stories I could tell you about my own kitchen disasters.

"My poor husband ate whatever I put in front of him whether it was burnt black as a boot strap or undercooked and inedible. He said he didn't care about my cooking 'cause he loved me and that was all that mattered. The man was a saint."

Sarah laughed at Flora's stories. "Quinn said much the same thing. He's a good man and I don't want to take advantage of his good heart." She gathered her courage and took a deep breath. "Flora, would you mind giving me some cooking lessons sometime? I'd really like to be a good wife to Quinn."

Flora stood and pulled Sarah into a big hug. "Of course, my dear. I would be honored and delighted to give you cooking lessons. You and this little family of yours is a godsend. Christmas is an especially hard time for me with my husband gone and all my family in St. Louis. You and Becca are an answer to my prayers. You are my Christmas miracles."

CHAPTER 17

Quinn stopped off at Ona's bakery after he left his beautiful wife sitting in a food coated kitchen. He bought enough fresh baked bread and applesauce donuts to keep Bishop from getting noisy about having a late breakfast.

He had also left his wife in a much better mood than when he found her. When he stepped inside their tiny kitchen this morning, his intentions were to find out what was keeping his prisoner's breakfast. Instead, he found out a whole lot more. *Sarah didn't know how to cook. She wanted to know if he could still love her.*

He wished he had had more time to show Sarah just how much he could love her, but he had a job to do and that prisoner of his was a real jackass. He would be so dang glad when that prison wagon made it through the mountain passes to pick his sorry ass up.

Quinn dropped the fresh baked bread and applesauce donuts off to his prisoner, then locked his office doors. He had a very important errand to run and he wanted to get it done as soon as possible.

He walked the few blocks to the telegraph office. He penned his message to his friend and handed it to the telegraph operator, Clarence Shaw.

"That'll be two bits, Sheriff." Clarence informed him.

He paid the man and leaned into the window. "This is a highly confidential message, Clarence. I trust you will keep the contents of this telegraph to yourself."

"Of course, Sheriff Cassidy. That's my job" The man stated matter-of-factly.

"Good. Let me know as soon as you get an answer, will you? Day or night."

"Yes, sir, Sheriff. Will do." Clarence assured him.

Quinn left the telegraph office and made his rounds, stopping in to visit Jack and give him an extra flake of hay. He patted the blue roan horse on the neck and scratched him behind his ears. "Hey, boy. How about a ride this afternoon? Would that feel good?"

Jack munched on his hay and leaned into Quinn's scratch.

"Goin' for a ride today, Sheriff?" Willie's head popped up from two stalls over, rake in hand.

"Yeah, Willie. Actually, I was thinking I might rent that draft horse and sleigh of yours to take Sarah and Becca out for a ride after lunch today. That is, if I can find someone to keep an eye on my prisoner while I'm gone."

Quinn watched the stable owner dig into his back pocket and pull out a plug of brown tobacco, break off a piece and stick it into his mouth. "I'd be happy to rent ol' Jasper to ya, Sheriff." The wiry man offered a plug of the tobacco to him. When Quinn declined, Willie shoved the tobacco back into his pocket. "I'm just about done with my mornin' chores. I'd be happy to hep ya out with that prisoner of yorn too, Sheriff."

"That's great news, Willie. I'll be back to pick up Jasper around twelve thirty."

"I'll have 'im ready." Willie assured him.

~

Two hours later, Quinn locked his office door and headed for home. He figured he should give his wife and daughter time to prepare for their first adventure into the mountains instead of just showing up at the front door with a sleigh hooked to a giant Belgium draft horse.

He took off his boots at the back door and quietly stepped inside his little kitchen on socked feet. Once again, he found himself dumb struck by the site that greeted him. Just like this morning, there was food—everywhere, but this time, something was different. The food was actually *in* the bowls instead of dripping from the ceiling. He couldn't help but grin.

He watched his wife and daughter in the middle of the kitchen surrounded by sacks of flour and sugar. Bowls covered every flat surface in the kitchen. It was the picture of a happy home. His happy home. *Another Christmas miracle.*

He walked up behind Sarah and grabbed her around the waist, spinning her around and gifting her with a toe-curling kiss.

"Quinn!" She slapped him on the arm although there was no ire behind it. "Becca's watching," she admonished.

Quinn was about to ask what was going on, when a familiar voice called out from the front parlor. "Sarah, where did you say you kept your cleaning rags?"

Flora Lawrence entered the kitchen and stopped short when she saw Sarah wrapped in his arms.

"Oh, I'm sorry, Mrs. Lawrence. I didn't know my wife had company. My apologies." Quinn stepped away from Sarah and tried to hide his embarrassment at being caught kissing his wife in the middle of the day.

Flora grinned at him. "No need to apologize to me, Sheriff. I know a happy husband when I see one." The widow took off her apron and grabbed her coat off the back of one of the kitchen chairs. "I think I'll head home now. Sarah, why don't you and I finish this cooking lesson on Monday?"

"Cooking lessons? Already? My, my. It seems when my wife puts her mind to something, she is not to be deterred." He wondered what other activities his wife's determination could improve upon.

Flora grinned at him and left through the front door. Becca's little voice interrupted his thoughts. "Does this mean we can't make our cookies today, Momma?"

He picked Becca up and twirled her around in his arms. He loved the sound of her girlish giggle and how it made him feel. Like her father.

"Well, I suppose it does, Becca." He knew he was grinning like an imbecile, but he didn't really care. "I was hoping, instead of baking cookies today, you, and your gorgeous mother, might be up for an adventure on this beautiful Saturday afternoon. But, I suppose if you have your heart set on making cookies—"

He put her down and she hugged his legs. "What kind of adventure? Tell me, Quinn. I want to know."

He lifted her into his arms again and grinned, rubbing his nose to hers. "I have a surprise. How about a ride into the woods in Willie's sleigh?" He cast a questioning look toward Sarah hoping to get her approval too.

"Why?" Becca wanted to know.

"We are going to find our perfect Christmas tree."

"What?" The little girl squirmed to get down and Quinn set her on the floor. "We're getting a Christmas tree? Oh, that's a wonderful surprise. I'm going to get dressed in my warmest stockings and boots. Can we build a snowman in the woods?" Becca called over her shoulder and disappeared through the door to her bedroom.

"It's a bit early to cut a Christmas tree, don't you think?" Sarah grinned at Quinn. "I guess that means no dessert for you today."

"I'll save room for dessert tonight. By then, Becca will be exhausted, and I'll have you all to myself. But to answer your question, it's never too early to lay claim to the perfect Christmas tree, especially when everyone else in Angel Creek will be trying to stake their claim too. Besides, I wanted to spend some quality time with my family. Anything wrong with that?"

Quinn pulled his wife into his arms and kissed her. He was delighted when she kissed him back. He wanted more but it would have to wait. He held her at arm's length. "If you keep looking at me like that, we are going to disappoint Becca."

Sarah grinned up at him. "No, there's nothing at all wrong with that. It sounds like a lovely idea. And, you are right. Becca would never let us forget it."

"No. I can guarantee you she would not." Quinn changed direction. "I rented Willie's draft and sleigh for the afternoon. I'll go get them and meet you out front in about half an hour. Dress warm."

The heat he saw in his wife's eyes almost made him change his mind about leaving the house at all today, but then there was Becca to think about. He couldn't—he wouldn't—disappoint his little girl.

He kissed Sarah again, this time he left no doubt as to his promise of things to come. Nightfall couldn't come soon enough for him. He pulled away and looked into the depths of her deep brown eyes. "Um, well, I guess I better get going or we are going to have a lot of explaining to do when Becca returns and there's no sleigh."

"I think you might be right." Sarah's breath feathered his throat at the opening of his shirt. A ripple of desire bolted south. "I gotta go."

Quinn left his house as soon as he could get his boots and coat back on. His excitement at spending the day with his family carried his tall frame to the stables in long quick strides.

True to his word, Willie had Jasper hitched to the sleigh. He had even saddled Jack and tied him to the back of the sleigh. Quinn wasn't planning to ride Jack, but the horse could use the exercise and he had learned long ago a wagon could break down in the most inappropriate place.

He checked to make certain Willie was tucked safe inside the jail to keep an eye on Bishop. Satisfied Willie could take care of himself, he stepped aboard the sleigh and slapped the leather reins against ole Jasper's rump. "Come on, boy. Let's pick up my family."

His family. That thought gave him such joy. He whistled a Christmas song at the prospect of spending the day in the beautiful pine forests with Sarah and Becca. It was his first Christmas as a husband and a father. He intended to do everything in his power to make it a magical time they would always look back on and remember how happy they were.

The sun was high in the blue, December sky when Quinn pulled up in front of his family's home. He looked down the street at Flora's house. There was something about that house that felt like home. He had asked the widow if she had thought anymore about selling it. Her answer was still maybe. That would have to do for now.

Sarah and Becca stepped out of the cozy little house they now called home, their cheeks flushed with excitement. It was going to be a glorious day. He stepped down and lifted Becca up and on to the broad bench seat. Then, he took Sarah's hand and helped her up too. He kissed her gloved hand and their eyes met. A jolt of desire for his beautiful wife hit him hard. Maybe Flora could watch Becca for a few hours—

"Are we gonna go cut a Christmas tree or not?" Becca complained.

Quinn grinned up at Sarah. "Yes, we are my little Christmas elf. Yes, we certainly are." He sent his wife a smoldering look. He intended it as a message to let her know they would pick up where he left off later. If that beautiful blush on her cheeks held any clues, she received his message loud and clear

The ride through the fragrant pine forests was a feast for one's senses. Fragrant pines filled the crisp cold air with the earthy smell of fresh pine needles. Snow sparkled with every motion they made through the woods. Fir, pine and bare aspen trees hung heavy with the white crystalline powder. His heart settled calm and peaceful inside his chest. This was heaven on earth.

"Quinn, this is so beautiful. Thank you for sharing this amazing sight with us." Sarah said, flashing a grateful smile.

"The pleasure is all mine." He smiled at his wife over the head of his little girl sitting between them.

"Quinn, I want a tree this big." Becca spread her arms as wide as she was able. "Can we get one that big?"

"Yes, we can get one even bigger, if that's what you want." Quinn promised.

Sarah laughed. "Remember we have to get that tree into our front room. It can't be too big, or we will be standing outside the house looking in to see the tree because there won't be room for us."

Quinn stole a look at his wife. He wished he could give her a bigger house for Christmas. When he got back to town, he would ask Flora Lawrence again if she had given anymore thought to selling her house to him. He really wanted that house for his family.

"Hurry, Quinn. Make the horse go faster. I want to find the perfect Christmas tree for our house. Santa will be so impressed, he will leave us lots and lots and lots of presents. Maybe he'll even bring me a puppy." The unbridled joy on Becca's face warmed Quinn's heart.

Quinn snapped the reins on the big draft horse's rump. The harness bells jingled, and he swore it played a Christmas tune. He raised his voice and started singing *O Tannenbaum*. He wasn't certain he had all the words right, but it didn't matter to him or his family. They joined him and made up their own words, singing the song at the top of their lungs until they saw it—the perfect Christmas tree.

CHAPTER 18

S ix weeks later, Quinn sat at his desk deep in thought. He still hadn't heard anything from his friend John whether there was an arrest warrant with Sarah's name on it, and he was getting worried.

A lot had happened around town since his bride and her friends arrived. Two strangers arrived in town a few weeks ago. Quinn suspected they were in town to help Johnny Bishop escape so he questioned them. As it turned out, one of the men was from Charleston trying to track down a woman named Charity—his friend Lewis's wife.

The man after her was Mike Devillin, and he admitted he worked for another gentleman from Charleston by the name of John Roberts. It turned out that man was no gentleman. He owned a brothel back in Charleston and he was accusing Sarah's friend of doing substantial damage to his property before she left town.

He sent a telegram to the federal marshal in Great Falls to see if this Devillin hombre was wanted for anything. He warned the man he had no jurisdiction in Montana Territory. If he didn't have a legal notice for collection, he wasn't going to get any help from Quinn, and if he pushed too far, he would be looking at the inside of a jail cell instead of Charity.

Then, there was the issue of the other man. It seems he was looking for his missing son and he accused Lewis of having something to do with his son's disappearance. It turned out Lewis and Charity had some pretty serious secrets of his own. He wondered if Matt, Levi and Trevor or their wives had secrets from each other? He supposed every married couple had something they held back.

As sheriff of Angel Creek, he made inquiries into Lewis's situation. He told Lewis he wouldn't arrest h im until he could either corroborate or refute his story. Things were shaping up to be one hell of a Christmas in Angel Creek this year.

A knock at the door pulled him from his morbid thoughts and Flora Lawrence stepped inside, her cheeks rosy from the cold. He stood and greeted her at the door.

"Good morning, Flora. What brings you by my jail so early this beautiful December morning? I'm not used to seeing you here since Sarah took over the feeding of my prisoner."

"Hello, Sheriff. It is a beautiful morning, isn't it? Do you have a moment to speak to me about a matter? I know Sarah is quilting with her friends at your house so I thought now might be a good time to talk.

Quinn ushered Flora to the chair next to his desk and took his seat. "Of course. You sound serious. Is there something troubling you?"

"No. Not troubling me, but I have been thinking a lot about your offer and I'm gonna take you up on it. If you still have a mind to, that is?"

Quinn wasn't following the woman's conversation. "Offer? What offer?"

Flora pinked in embarrassment. "I must have misunderstood, Quinn. I thought you were interested in buying my house. I've decided to move back to St. Louis and live with my sister for a spell—"

He jumped up and pulled the Widow Lawrence out of her chair and spun her around the room. "Of course, I'm interested. I'm one hundred percent interested. Just name your price."

The widow's offer was unexpected and it caught him off guard, but he was no less excited to hear her news. He spun her around again and kissed her on the cheek just as Sarah walked into the office. She had his prisoner's breakfast in the basket hanging over her arm.

Quinn's laughter died off at his wife's startled expression, and he and the widow stood side-by-side in embarrassed silence.

He felt he need to say something. "Sarah, I can explain. Me and Flora here—I mean Mrs. Lawrence, we were—"

A smile softened his wife's frown. She set the basket of food down on the top of his desk and turned to face him.

"There's no need to explain, Quinn. No need at all. I assume there's a very good reason my husband is kissing one of my best friend's and spinning her in the air. Care to share?" Sarah grinned her eyebrows raised in question.

Quinn grinned back at his beautiful wife. "I have some marvelous news I think you are going to absolutely love. Flora has decided to move back to St. Louis—"

"That's horrible news, Quinn. How could you behave this way, and in front of Flora?" His wife walked toward her friend. "I'm so sorry, Flora. I don't know what's gotten into this husband of mine this morning." Sarah wrapped an arm around Flora's shoulder to comfort her.

Flora nodded. "Why don't I let him tell you the news." She hugged Sarah back and turned to him. "Quinn, stop by the bank later this afternoon. I'll make certain everything is in order and you can just wire the money to the bank in St. Louis, if that's agreeable to you.

"Now, I have to go. Prudence has nagged me to death for my cinnamon roll recipe. I'm going to give it to her as a Christmas present, but don't tell her I'm also giving it to you, Sarah. Prudence Bailey is a dear friend, but she's a bit of a snoot when it comes to her baking. I can't wait to watch you outshine her when you make my famous cinnamon rolls. It'll be good to see you take her down a peg or two."

Flora left his office and him alone with his bride.

"Quinn, what is going on? Why is Flora leaving and what are you giving her money for? Has something happened?" He couldn't stand his wife's beautiful face etched with worry. He didn't waste any time in telling her the news.

"Sarah, Flora is moving to St. Louis to live with her sister and she agreed to sell me—us—her house." Quinn stood back and grinned at his wife. Her reaction wasn't the one he expected.

"You mean, we aren't going to live in our cozy little home anymore?"

Sarah didn't seem as excited as he had hoped. "Um, well, no. I mean, I thought you'd be excited to have a bigger house. You know, more room and a bigger kitchen, but from your reaction it seems I was wrong."

Quinn squelched his disappointment. He thought his little southern belle would be delighted not to have to hang her dresses on pegs on the wall or bath in the kitchen near the fire.

"Quinn, tell me why you bought the house." His wife searched his face. What was she looking for?

"I bought it because I thought you would like it, you know, a bigger place. And so Becca could have her own room. You've done such a wonderful job of making that rough pile of wooden planks into a home, but I guess I wanted to give you the things you are missing from your old life in Charleston—"

She placed a finger over his lips to quiet him. "Quinn, there's nothing I miss from my old life and nothing I would trade one moment of my life here with you. Nothing at all. Not the big mansions. Not the extravagant dresses. Not someone to draw my bath or cook my food. I love you, Quinn, and I want nothing more from this life than to live it with you by my side, wherever that may be."

He saw tears of love shining in his wife's sultry eyes. *She loved him.* He was the luckiest man on this earth. He pulled her to him and leaned in to kiss her. The feel of her body, warm and soft, under her winter clothing never failed to make him wish for night fall.

"Sheriff, when do I get my breakfast? I smell food but it ain't appeared yet and I'm durn near starved to death." His prisoner yelled from his cell.

"Damn it, Bishop—" Quinn started to pay the man a visit. Sarah stayed him with her hand.

"Quinn, he's only gonna be here one more day. It would be a shame to let him spoil your stellar record as a lawman on his last day. I'll take him his breakfast. Then you and I can talk about how much money I get to spend on decorating Flora's—I mean—*our* new home."

"Are you saying you want to live in Flora's house." Quinn's heart stuttered in anticipation.

"I'm saying, I want to live where you live, and if that happens to be the beautiful two-story house down the street with the white picket fence and the big bay window just the right size for the perfect Christmas tree with a very large bedroom upstairs," his wife wiggled her eyebrows in his direction, "then yes, that's what I'm saying."

His wife blew him a kiss just before she disappeared behind the door to Bishop's cell.

Quinn couldn't stop grinning. "Well, hot damn."

∿

Sarah was thrilled when she kissed Quinn goodbye at his office and hurried home to make Becca breakfast. He had bought *her* a house. No one had ever put her needs before their own. Certainly not William, that much was certain.

When she had seen Quinn swinging Flora around this morning and kissing her on the cheek, she had to admit that ugly green monster of jealousy reared its ugly head, but just for a moment. She knew without a shadow of a doubt, Quinn was a good man. An honorable man. And she loved him with all of her heart and soul. More importantly, she trusted him.

When he told her about the house, she wished she could have brought him home and thanked him properly. She had been sorely tempted, but her friends Anna and Charity, were coming to her house this morning to work on their community project for Christmas. She would save her thanks to her husband for later when the night grew still and Becca was fast asleep.

Becca finished eating just as some of her classmates arrived at the front door to whisk her off to school. Her daughter loved her studies and her classmates and she had been so excited when her teacher, Mrs. Schultz chose her as one of the children to sing at the Christmas Eve party.

An old pro at baking now, Sarah stood in her tiny kitchen and mixed together the ingredients for Flora's recipe for sugar cookies and placed them on a tin sheet and placed them in the oven. She had been so excited when Flora told her she would gift her the precious recipe for her cinnamon rolls. She would do her very best to live up to the famed pastries.

She put the finishing touches on her cookies and the house smelled of fresh baked cookies when Anna and Charity arrived at her doorstep. Ever since her first cooking lesson with Flora, she had used them as her taste testers. Not only did Quinn eat her experiments, so did her dear friends.

"Hello, come in. It's cold outside." Sarah ushered Anna and Charity inside and closed the door against the frigid winter air.

"Sit down. I have a new recipe I'm trying out on you today. " She placed the plate of cookies in front of them.

Charity grinned and grabbed a cookie. "If you keep this up, I'm going to be two axle handles wide."

Anna agreed. "Me too." She mumbled through the bite of cookie in her mouth.

After catching up with each other's lives, she and her friends worked through the rest of the morning and put the finishing touches on the quilts they were making for Angel Creek's less fortunate families.

Sarah's mind wandered from the conversations when she felt her baby move in her belly. Quinn was going to be so excited when she told him about—

"Sarah, are you listening to me?" Charity asked.

"Yes, yes, of course. I—no, not exactly. I'm sorry. My mind was wandering. What were you saying?" Sarah turned to her friend with a sheepish grin.

"I asked you what you got Quinn for Christmas."

"Yeah, is it a big secret?" Anna asked.

She wasn't ready to share her news about the baby with her friends—not until she had the opportunity to tell Quinn, so she told her friends about the silver conches under the tree. "I got him something for his horse. He loves that horse." Sarah offered.

"Do you know what he got you?" Anna asked and helped herself to another cinnamon roll.

"Well, he did buy me a house so I think it would be ungracious of me to expect more. I told him I had everything I could possibly want." Sarah thought about the baby growing in her belly. "Absolutely everything."

"Yeah, I think we've all been a bit surprised by our luck. Who knew we would find such a happy life by answering an advertisement for wives in a newspaper. Why, it's unheard of, don't you think?" Charity stood and began picking up the spools of thread and putting them back into Sarah's sewing basket.

Anna agreed. "I never would have and yet, we all must have had some inkling. Why else would we have come all this way to marry total strangers?"

"Yes, I suppose that's true to some degree." Sarah admitted. "Does anyone want another cinnamon roll? I have a whole pan full in the kitchen."

Charity stood to leave. "No, I need to get back to the saloon. Lewis is waiting on me and we have a lot to talk about."

Anna stood to go too. "Yeah, I need to get home before Levi comes looking for me as well."

Sarah stood and accompanied her friends to the door. "I'll see you both at the Christmas Eve party tomorrow. And to think, this time next week, I'll be in a new house with plenty of room for Anna's quilting frame and we'll have a kitchen big enough to bake baskets and baskets of food. Since Flora is leaving Angel Creek, I thought I'd take over her efforts to feed those less fortunate."

Anna and Charity looked at each other and then turned back to her and burst out laughing.

"What's so funny?" Sarah had no idea why her friends were laughing.

"You. Talking about cooking. It hasn't been that long you were trying to figure out a way not to tell your husband you didn't know how to cook. Now, you are cooking every day." Charity offered in explanation.

Sarah blushed. "Yes, I suppose we've all come a long way from Charleston."

"In more ways than just the miles, that's for certain." Anna added.

"Momma, when is Quinn coming to get me?" Becca's voice called out to her from her bedroom. "He promised to take me Christmas shopping today so I can buy my teacher a present before we sing tomorrow."

"He'll be here soon, Becca. He's at work, remember? I'd better go before she decides to go hunt him down." Sarah hugged her friends and closed the door behind them. She thought about what Anna had said. They all had come such a long way and it wasn't just about the miles that lay between Angel Creek and Charleston.

The change between Becca when she first arrived and Becca now was profound. Every night, Becca insisted both she and Quinn read her a bedtime story. He didn't seem to mind at all cuddling up with Becca on her tiny bed and reading to her.

Sarah was just grateful the stories her daughter chose most nights were short, because she had a very hard time keeping her hands off her handsome husband. And tonight, after the Christmas Eve party, when Becca was fast asleep, she would pull her husband close and tell him about their Christmas miracle growing inside her.

Sarah sat in her tiny living room amidst the quilting frame and bolts of muslin and cotton batting. Spools of thread lined her sewing basket. Ornaments and boughs of pine adorning the fireplace mantle. It was going to be her best Christmas ever.

She picked up the beautiful silver Conchos she had purchased from the mercantile store. Mr. Weston said they would be easy to add to Jack's bridle. Sarah knew how much Quinn loved that horse and she wanted to give him something that was just for him. He had given her so much already.

Sarah smiled to herself. She was such a lucky woman. Thoughts of all those nights safe and warm in Quinn's arms made her blush. It was during one of those nights Quinn shared the contents of his little trunk of treasures she and Becca had found when they cleaned out the storage room to make her bedroom. She and Quinn lay together side-by-side going through his past long after Becca was asleep.

Picture by picture, Sarah learned about her husband and his family. His losses. His heartaches. His parents, his brothers, both when they were young and all grown up in military dress. He shared his past with Sarah and she understood his side of the war—the war she had once blamed him for.

She fingered her mother's necklace she still wore around her neck. It was a reminder of her past—one she thought she couldn't live without. That was before she found her future. With Quinn

And now, despite what Quinn believed about his inability to father children, the tiny baby bump she hid beneath her winter skirts told a different story. She couldn't wait to tell Quinn that his surgeon was wrong. Very, very wrong.

CHAPTER 19

*Q*uinn sat in his office and racked his brain. What on earth was he going to get his wife for Christmas? Tomorrow was the town's Christmas Eve party and he still hadn't bought Sarah anything at all.

When he had asked her for a hint at what she might like, she had told him he had already given her everything she could ever want. For a woman who came from a wealthy background, she put very little demands on his money even though he had it to give.

He had been surprised when he had written to the overseer of his family's estate asking to withdraw money so he could buy Flora's house. He knew there would be enough money for the purchase, but he had no idea just how much the estate had grown in his absence.

When his brothers were killed, and his parents died, he was left as the sole heir. He hadn't wanted anything to do with it at the time. It was a painful reminder that his family was gone. His mother. His father. His brothers. All gone.

But now, he had a new family and he wanted them to have everything he could provide for them. He offered Sarah the opportunity to move to New York into his family's estate. She declined and assured him over and over she wanted to live out her days in Angel Creek. With her daughter. With her friends. With him in the house of their dreams.

He just wished he knew what Sarah's future held. Still no word from John Mallory and that was making him very nervous. He could buy her all the houses in the world but the one thing he couldn't buy her was her freedom if bad luck came knocking on their door.

As if his thoughts conjured the knock, Curtis Carter, Angel Creek's postman of sorts, stepped inside. "Good morning, Sheriff. The mail coach just arrived. Here's some packages for you."

"Thank you, Curtis." Quinn took the packets from the man and offered him a cup of coffee.

"No thanks, Sheriff. I got a lot of packages waiting on me to deliver. Christmas is right around the corner and people are countin' on me. Better get to it." Curtis tipped his hat and left.

Quinn recognized the top packet. It was would be full of new wanted posters. His heart always skipped an extra beat when he ripped open the package and spread them across his desk. He prayed each time the packet arrived he wouldn't see his beautiful wife's face on one of them.

Usually, he didn't get much mail, but today, there was another package on his desk. He turned it over. His heart stuttered and stalled. It was addressed to him from— *John Mallory, New York City, New York.*

Quinn's hands shook when he ripped the package open. A handful of papers fell to the floor. He anxiously scooped them up and piled them on his desk. His friend's distinctive handwriting appeared on one of the pages. He pulled the letter out of the stack and began to read. John didn't waste any time with pleasantries.

. . .

"Dear Quinn,

Enclosed with my letter are several newspaper articles I thought you might find interesting about your wife's family. Unfortunately, there is also a copy of an official arrest warrant with your wife's name on it. Steady, Quinn. I know you, and you are already trying to figure out a way to keep your wife safe without compromising your integrity. Before you go off half-cocked, keep reading.

Your wife's in-laws were killed in an attempted robbery about three weeks ago. That would seem tragic except the situation isn't as simple as it would appear on the surface. The irony of the situation is Mr. and Mrs. Caldwell were leaving the country with a lot of valuable goods which is why they were targeted for robbery in the first place. As it turns out, the items in their possession didn't belong to them.

The illustrious Mr. Caldwell had been embezzling money from his so-called friends for quite some time. He and his wife had planned their escape and purchased two one-way tickets on a steamer to Europe.

In your packet is the Caldwell's robbery report. The investigating federal marshal included all the details about the robbery, and a few more facts I think you'll find quite interesting. Flip to Page Two and you'll see testimony from a woman who worked for the Caldwells. Her name is Agatha Handy.

She told the marshal what the Caldwells had done to obtain custody of your wife's daughter, Rebecca. The marshal presented evidence to a judge with jurisdiction to hear the case. The judge declared the arrest warrant invalid. That means your wife is a free woman, Quinn.

The rest of the documents in the packet are of a legal nature I thought your wife might want. Death certificates. Wills. Bank accounts. Caldwell holdings. As you can see, there's nothing of any value there, so I'm sorry I couldn't give you better news there. And the Handy woman asked if I would give your wife her note. It's in the packet too.

Consider this news as my Christmas present to you. If you should be so inclined to send me a Christmas present in return, I wouldn't be upset in the least to find that blue roan horse of yours on my door step. Since I know that isn't going to happen, I'd be satisfied to see you again, and meet your family. Merry Christmas and much happiness to you, Quinn. You deserve it.

Your friend,

John

Quinn leaned back in his chair and read John's letter again. He breathed a happy sigh of relief. So, it was true. Sarah wasn't wanted by the law. Another Christmas miracle to be thankful for.

He gathered the papers and stuffed them into the packet. He poked his head inside the cell area to check on his prisoner. The man was playing cards on his bunk. "Bishop. Don't get into any trouble while I'm gone. I've got an errand that can't wait another minute." He grinned at his own joke.

"Well, what the hell am I gonna do to get in trouble in here, Sheriff?" The man never looked up from his game.

Quinn locked his office door and headed for home. He couldn't wait to tell his beautiful wife the good news.

"Merry Christmas, darling."

Sarah had never been happier in her life. Not even her best days in Charleston could compare with her life here in Angel Creek. Today was Christmas Eve. Sarah sat in her tiny living room with her friends, Charity, Anna, and Julia putting the last-minute touches on their Christmas quilts.

It was a task she had seen time and time again back home in Charleston. She thought the task tedious and mundane, but now she understood its purpose. It wasn't just the act of sewing something to keep a person warm. No, it was about the connection between friends. The love between souls who weren't connected by blood. And it was about the memories of time spent with those special people.

When Quinn had come home yesterday and handed her the packet from his friend, she thought she would swoon. Her nightmare with the Caldwells was finally over and she had Mrs. Handy to thank for it all.

She read the letter of apology from William's aged nanny. It seems she was as much a victim of the Caldwell's as she. They threatened to put her out of their home without the pension they had promised her for so many years if she didn't go along with their plans. It was the only reason she had stayed after William left home. And the only reason she kept Becca from Sarah that day. She asked for Sarah's forgiveness and prayed for Sarah and Becca's happiness.

Sarah was happy to oblige the woman. She held no ill will toward Mrs. Handy. If anything, she owed the woman a huge debt of gratitude for coming forward and telling the truth. She hated to think what could have happened had she not.

The last six weeks living in Angel Creek, surrounded by community, family and a sense of belonging, was heaven on earth for Sarah, but it was her nights in the arms of her handsome lawman husband that gave her life new meaning. He knew all of her secrets and he still loved her.

For the first time in Sarah's twenty-seven years, she felt as if she belonged somewhere. Really belonged. Not because of her last name or how much wealth her family had. No, she belonged because she had a purpose in this tight knit community. She was contributing to the greater cause with her own skills and hard work. And it felt good.

CHAPTER 20

uinn still hadn't gotten Sarah anything for
Christmas and the town's Christmas Eve party was
tonight. After he had rushed home yesterday and
told her about the packet he had received from his friend,
they had jumped for joy and then jumped into each other's
arms.

He had left the house this morning to check on Eugene
and his prisoner. Today was the day Bishop would be leaving
Angel Creek courtesy of the prison wagon. He couldn't say
he was sorry to see the man go either.

Eugene said he would be happy to stay a little while
longer this morning so he and Becca could go Christmas
shopping. Quinn hurried home to find Becca waiting for
him. The little girl rushed him at the door smothering him
with kisses, hugs and questions. Her excitement was conta-
gious and Quinn couldn't wait until Christmas morning
when Becca found her new puppy under the tree.

An hour later, he and Becca stepped out of the Weston's
mercantile, arms full of packages. He looked down at the

excited little girl beside to him. Her cheeks flushed rosy pink with the cold air, lit up her face. Her blue eyes danced with excitement. "Quinn, what time does Santa come tonight?"

"Becca, he will only come when you are fast asleep." Quinn assured her.

"But why does he only come when I'm asleep? I want to talk to him." Becca's innocent question caught him off guard.

"What do you want to talk to him about?" Quinn jostled his packages in his other arm and held Becca's hand while they crossed the busy street and headed for his office. He wanted to finish up his paperwork for the transfer of his prisoner before the party tonight. He didn't want anything spoiling his family's fun.

Quinn crossed the street and he let go Becca's hand. She skipped a few feet ahead of him working hard to miss the cracks in the boardwalk. He wondered what more this little daughter of his could wish for. "Becca, honey, you don't have any more room in your little room for more toys. Or books. I know when we move into the Widow Lawrence's house, you'll have more room, but—

"Oh, I don't want to ask him for more toys, Quinn. I want to ask him to bring warm socks and mittens for Jessie Baylor in my class. Oh, and boots. He comes to school with holes in his shoes and he's always shivering from the cold. I asked Momma to bake him some cinnamum rolls too. He's always so hungry—"

Quinn's heart melted at his little daughter's words. She wanted to ask for warm clothes and food for her classmate. He could make that happen and as soon as he was finished here—he reached for his office door and stepped inside.

The sight in front of him stopped his heart. Eugene was standing next to the coffee pot, his arms raised in surrender while Johnny Bishop was standing in the doorway between his office and the jail cells, a gun now pointed at him. *And Becca.*

"Aww, now Sheriff. You didn't have to brang me no Christmas presents, but iffin' you don't mind, set 'em down right there on your desk so I can see your hands."

Quinn's instincts kicked in. He pushed Becca behind him and shot a look to his deputy. The look of chagrin on Eugene's face spoke volumes.

"Sure thing, Bishop." He set the presents down on his desk and turned his attention back to the man with the gun.

"I knowed you is a smart man so don't do nothin' stupid 'cause I'd had to shoot yer depety or that little girl of yourn, but I will. As God is my witness, I'll do it if you try to stop me from getting' outta here. Now shut that front door and slide that Colt of yourn across the floor."

"Good morning, Johnny." He did his best to keep his voice steady through his terror at having Becca in the middle of all this. He had to keep his head about him to prevent anyone from getting hurt. Or worse. He unbuckled his holster and slide it across the floor.

"What's the matter, Johnny Boy? Wasn't my wife's cookin' up to your standards? Let's talk about this and see what we can come up with to make it better." He spoke to his escaping prisoner as he would a frightened colt even though John Bishop was more like a cornered wolf. The man had killed before. He would do it again if he had to. Quinn would need every ounce of his military finesse to get them all out of this mess.

"It was passable, Sheriff. I ain't got no complaints. That ain't it and you knowed it. I heard the prison wagon arrived last night and I ain't getting' on it." The man raised the gun toward him and toed Quinn's closer. He reached down and picked up the gun and stuffed into the waistband of his britches. Quinn felt naked without the peacemaker in his hand. Damn it. He had let his guard down and now look what was happening right before his eyes.

"Johnny, the federal marshal and his deputies are just across the street. If you fire that gun, you don't stand a chance in hell at getting' outta here alive. Why don't we talk about this. I'm sure I can figure something—"

"Ain't nothin' to figga out, Sheriff. I'm leavin' and if you try to stop me, somebody's gonna get hurt."

It was at that moment, the front door of the office opened and his beautiful wife stepped in with a basket full of breakfast for his prisoner—who was now free to kill his family. Sarah's shocked look and the fear in her eyes made him sick at his stomach. His job was to protect his family, not put them in harm's way.

"Well, look who we have here." Johnny Bishop's perusal of his wife made Quinn's skin crawl. "Hello, pretty lady. Whatcha got in that basket for ole' Johnny this morning? Step inside and close that door behind ya. Don't want no unwanted guests gobblin' up my food, now do we?"

Sarah shot Quinn a look. Her meaning was impossible to miss. She was scared to death for him and her daughter. Quinn knew it was up to him to get them out of this mess. "It's okay, Sarah. Everything is going to be alright. Set the basket on my desk and you and Becca head home—"

"Not so fast, Sheriff. Are you trying to pull a fast one on me? They ain't going nowhere. They is my insurance policy of getting' outta here."

"No, I'm your insurance policy, Bishop. I'll give you my horse and escort you out of town. No tricks, but if you think I'm gonna let you walk out of here with my wife and daughter as your hostages, I'll kill you with my bare hands where you stand first."

Bishop shot a calculating look to him and then to Becca

and Sarah. "I'll take my chances, Sheriff. You is too much trouble. And, as much as I would like to spend some time with that beautiful wife a yorn, I'd have to watch her too close. Wouldn't be able to sleep none for fear she'd bash my head in with an iron skillet."

He waved Quinn and Sarah over to stand next to Eugene. Quinn reached for Becca who was still hiding behind him when Johnny shook his head no. "Huh uh, Sheriff. She stays right where she is."

"Bishop—" Quinn shielded Sarah behind him and they moved to stand next to Eugene. He felt Sarah's frightened sobs against his back. She was clinging to him. She had put her trust, her faith and her love in him. He would die before he let her and Becca down. "What's your plan, Bishop? Are you gonna put a little girl between you and a bullet?"

"I don't want nobody else to die on accounta me, Sheriff. That's the God's truth, but I ain't getting' on that prison wagon. My plan is this and youse is gonna go along with it or —well, I don't think I have to spell out the consequences, now do I?"

Bishop kept his back to the wall and his gun pointed on the three of them while he inched closer and closer to Becca.

"Quinn?" Sarah whispered from behind him. He could feel her tremble against his back. "Sarah, stay calm. I'll take care of this. I promise." He reached behind him and found her hand and squeezed it.

She lay her cheek against his coat and squeezed his hand back. "I trust you, Quinn. Please be careful." She whispered.

Her faith in him gave him the calm courage he needed to think this situation through . He and Sarah and Becca had come too far to lose everything now.

"Bishop, you aren't gonna get ten feet out that door. The marshal's deputies are standing guard down the street. Let me help you and nobody has to get hurt." Quinn pleaded with the man.

Quinn saw the hesitation in the man's face. He knew he had planted a seed of doubt in the man's bravado. "Let me go with you."

"Naw, Sheriff—"

"You can wear Eugene's coat and hat. You can keep your gun in my back. I'll act like we are just making my usual rounds. Keep your hat pulled down over your face and I'll act like nothin's wrong. I can walk you down the street to the stables and I'll even give you my own horse to ride outta town on."

Quinn could see the shrewd interest on Bishop's face. He knew he had the man hooked, but the man was not stupid. One who lived a life of crime didn't live as long as Bishop had by being stupid.

"Lock them up in my cell, 'cause they ain't gonna be no chance in hell for me if they run off yellin' to the marshal as soon as we clear the door."

"Okay." He took a deep breath. "Becca, why don't you go to your momma? We are gonna play a game where you and your momma and Eugene hide in the cell and—"

"Huh uh, Sheriff. That little girl goes with us. I ain't taking no chances of you trying to wrestle this here gun outta my hand once we get within sight of those deputies outside. I know you ain't gonna do nothing to put that little girl of yours at risk."

Bishop pointed the gun in Sarah and Eugene's direction. "You two. Get inside my cell and lock the door behind ya." They both hurried into the back cells and Quinn heard the heavy iron door clang shut. Sarah's soft sobs punched him in the gut. "Now throw that dang key a yourn out here where I can see it."

Eugene's key skidded on the floor stopping next to the pot-bellied stove.

Bishop grinned and nodded. He stepped closer to Becca talking to her sweet and low as he put himself—and his gun—between Quinn and Becca. "Hey little dawlin', now don't you be afraid none. Me and your daddy's gonna take you for a walk around town." The man never took his eyes off Quinn.

Quinn's gaze never left Becca. Her little bottom lip trembled and her clear blue eyes looked to him for direction.

"It's okay, Becca. I'll be right there with you. I'll be holding your hand the whole time. Don't worry."

Quinn turned to Bishop. "You do something stupid and get my daughter hurt and you won't be able to ride fast enough or far enough to outrun me. You hear me, Bishop?" He growled at the man who was putting his whole future at risk.

"You don't do nothing stupid, lawman, and you won't have nothing to worry about. Now get moving." He pulled Eugene's hat and coat from the coat rack near the front door and put them on never allowing Quinn out of his sight.

Quinn took Becca's hand and squeezed it tight. "Don't worry, sweetheart. Everything is going to be okay. I promise." He prayed with all his heart he could keep that promise to his daughter and his wife.

He gripped Becca's hand tight and opened the door to his office. They stepped out on to the boardwalk and headed straight to the stables down the street. He knew Bishop was right behind him because he felt the barrel of the gun in his ribs.

Quinn nodded and waved to two deputies at the end of the block, standing guard at the prison wagon and harnessing up the team of eight draft horses used to pull the heavy contraption through the steep mountain trails.

One of the deputies called out to him. "Morning, Sheriff. Looks like it's gonna be a beautiful day."

"I hope you're right, Deputy. I sure hope you're right." Quinn called back.

Bishop pushed his gun deeper into his ribs. "Don't get too friendly, Sheriff. It might not end well for you and this here little girl of yourn."

Quinn kept a steady pace across the street toward the stables. Becca's hand held tight to his. Soon, they entered the dim stables. The tangy smell of horse urine and manure calmed his nerves a bit. Jack must have sensed his presence. His horse let out a loud whiney.

"Must be yourn horse, Sheriff. Saddle 'em up. Quick like." Bishop looked around the stable with suspicion. Quinn hurried inside Jack's stall taking Becca with him.

He made quick work of tacking up his horse. He led Jack out into the center aisle and offered the reins to Bishop. "Here. Take him. He's a good horse. He's not as fast as he used to be but he's sure-footed. He's exactly what you need in the rough terrain surrounding this town, and he's the only chance you've got."

"Not exactly, Sheriff. Now put that kid up on that saddle." Bishop shot a look over his shoulder for any problems. Everything was quiet.

"No. Bishop. That's where I draw the line. I'm not putting my daughter on a horse with you knowing you are going to ride hard from the law. If there's any shots fired, she could be the one hit. It isn't gonna happen, Bishop. Take your chances with the horse, 'cause you'll have to kill me to get my daughter. I'm not putting Becca on that horse."

The man's true nature finally made its appearance. His eyes grew hard and he bared his teeth. "You put that gol darn kid up on that horse or I'm gonna kill the both of you right here."

"Sure, Bishop. You do that. And those two deputies and the federal marshal will be waiting on you just outside that door. Then what? You're a dead man. Live or die don't matter to me, Bishop, but I'm telling you, I'm not putting my kid on that horse."

Quinn pulled Becca to him and pushed her behind him. If Bishop was gonna start shooting, he'd have to shoot through Quinn to get to Becca. He met the man's eyes with equal determination. He hoped his outright refusal would goad the man into just leaving.

He could see Bishop weighing his options when the ring of a metal shovel hitting bone reverberated through the stables. Bishop's stunned gaze glazed over just before he fell to the dirt and manure covered stall floor underneath Jack's legs.

The old war horse snorted and stepped sideways to avoid stepping on the man's body. Quinn held tight to the reins and pressed Becca against his side to keep her safe from Jack's stomping hooves.

Willie stepped out of the stall next to Jack's and stood over Bishop's unconscious body. "I was getting ready to clean out Jack's stall when I heard you come in, Sheriff. When I seen that man with a gun to your back and you with little Becca there, I knew somethin' bad was up right away. I hid and waited for my chance to bash him in the head. I did good, didn't I Sheriff?"

Quinn grinned and slapped Willie on the back. "You damn sure did, Willie, my friend. You damn sure did."

Becca stepped from behind him, hands on hips. "Quinn, you said damn again. You aren't supposed to say that word. Momma's gonna be mad at you."

Relief flooded Quinn. Everything was going to be okay now. "Well, then I think we should go and tell her what I did so I can say I'm sorry."

He picked up his daughter and spun her around, loving the sound of her girlish giggle. Setting her high up on Jack's saddle, he led them out of the stables and straight to federal deputies to inform them that the prisoner they were looking for was taking a nap in the stable. Then he headed straight for his office—and his wife.

EPILOGUE

A scream woke Sarah from a dead sleep. She bolted upright in bed—her heart in her throat—her feet hit the cold floor before she was fully awake. She had almost cleared the bed before her husband's voice of calm slowed her flight of fright.

"It's alright, Sarah. It's Christmas morning and I believe that scream was our daughter's joy at the discovery of her new puppy. Get ready—"

Quinn hadn't finished his sentence when Becca stormed through their bedroom door with a squirming bundle of black and tan spots.

"Look, Momma. Santa brought me a damn puppy. Can you believe it? Oh, I'm so happy. Hurry and get up. There's more presents under the tree." Becca left as quickly as she arrived leaving Sarah and Quinn to marvel at the joys of parenthood.

Sarah shot her husband a look of shocked amusement. "Did my daughter just say a curse word?"

She really should be upset that Quinn was teaching her proper little southern belle curse words, and she would definitely work on getting that bad habit stopped, but the cute look of chagrin on her handsome husband's face made her want to close the door and kiss him—all over.

"Merry Christmas, sweetheart?" He offered.

She grinned a wide happy grin and pulled him to her. He grinned back and gifted her with his very special good morning kiss, so soft and sweet it made her toes curl underneath the mound of bedcovers.

"Merry Christmas to you too, Quinn." Sarah whispered, her emotions all over the place. She didn't know if it was the baby or that she came so close to losing everything during yesterday's near catastrophe with Bishop. The sight of that man holding a gun on her husband and daughter—she didn't want to ever think about what could have happened if Quinn hadn't known what to do.

She was so happy when Quinn returned with Becca safe and sound to let them out of that jail cell, but when the federal marshal and his deputies loaded Bishop, and that Mr. Devillin that had been bothering Charity, on to that prison wagon in chains, she cried with joy.

"Momma! Daddy! Are you coming to see what Santa brought?" Becca's excited voice from the main room vibrated through the little house's plain board walls. Sarah watched her husband's eyes round in surprise at her daughter's words.

"Did she just call me—daddy?" Quinn asked in disbelief. "Did you tell her to say that, because if you did, I don't want—"

Sarah sat up in bed. "I swear, Quinn, I haven't even spoken to Becca about what she should call you. This is all her doing."

She watched her husband's face. "She called me daddy, Sarah." His voice whispered with emotion.

Sarah knew being a father meant so much to Quinn. He had chosen her because she had a child and he thought he couldn't—maybe now was a good time to tell him about the baby.

"Quinn, there's something I've wanted to tell you for a few weeks now, but I wanted to be sure before I said anything considering…."

Concern etched frown lines across her husband's handsome face. He pulled her to him and searched her face. She reached her hand and touched the white scar on his jaw. "Considering what, Sarah?"

"Quinn, do you remember when you told me the surgeon said you were too severely injured to father children?"

"Yes, I remember. Why bring that up now, Sarah?" she could see the pain on her husband's face at the mention of it.

"And, do you remember what I said to you when you told me?" She teased.

"Yes. You said it's one man's word against another man's determination."

"And I told you I was certain if you put your mind to it, you would prove that surgeon wrong."

"Yes, I remember, but what has that got to do—"

Quinn stopped short and pulled her to him. He searched her face, hope in his eyes. "What are you saying, Sarah? Are you telling me that you—we—that I am going to be a—" He couldn't seem to say the words.

"Yes, Quinn. We are going to have a baby." She whispered to him.

"Are you sure? I mean—are you absolutely certain?" Sarah touched his hand and placed it against her growing belly. "I am most assuredly positively absolutely certain. Merry Christmas, darling."

Her eyes filled with tears of joy as she watched her husband's own emotions crumble his handsome face. He hid his face in the crook of her neck and gently caressed her belly with his hand again.

"It's a good thing we are moving into Flora's house next week. The baby—our baby—" Quinn's reverent whisper underscored his shock at the news "would have had to sleep in a dresser drawer otherwise. I never would have even hoped for—"

"This little baby is our Christmas miracle, Quinn."

"No. It was the advertisement in the newspaper that was our Christmas miracle, Sarah. If it hadn't been for that ad, we wouldn't have found each other and we wouldn't be a family and we wouldn't be having this baby. I love you, Sarah Cassidy."

"Daddy! Momma! Get up! It's time to open our presents. Uh oh. The puppy peed on the floor." Becca's voice called out to them. "Ewwwwwww."

Quinn kissed her on the lips and got out of bed. He grabbed his pants and shirt from the floor where they had landed last night after they got home from the Christmas Eve party and Becca was fast asleep dreaming about Santa's visit. "I better get in there before we have a real mess on our hands."

He kissed her again and kissed her belly beneath the bedcovers. On his way out the door, he gifted her with that cheeky grin of his that always held the promise of more to come.

She snuggled deep into the warmth of her bed and listened to her husband and daughter laughing with delight. "Oh, there will be more to come, my dear husband. I can promise you that."

~

Christmas Eve, 1914
    Angel Creek, Montana

. . .

"Mother?" Sarah heard someone calling to her from far away. "Are you alright, Mother?"

Sarah's tired eyes opened to gaze upon the face of her youngest son, Colin. Named after one of Quinn's brothers lost in the war, he looked so much like his father. Strong. Handsome. Brave. His golden eyes and dark hair sometimes caused her heart to hiccup in her chest. Or maybe it was the shiny sheriff's badge pinned to his vest that made her forget for just a moment her beloved Quinn was gone.

"Of course, I'm alright. I just got lost in my memories for a bit. The retelling of how my friends and I came to Angel Creek does that to me sometimes—takes me back to the day I met and married your father. That's all." She squeezed his hand to reassure him.

He nodded in understanding and squeezed her hand back. "And your children never grow tired of hearing it—all six of us."

Sarah nodded. "I never get tired of telling it. Now, I think it's someone else's turn to tell her story. Anna, where are you?"

"I'm here, Sarah." Anna called from somewhere in the room. Sarah settled back in her chair and looked around the room one more time. The house that Quinn had bought for her was brimming with family and her very best friends in the whole world. She had so much to be thankful for this Christmas. So much. And yet—the one person she longed for was just out of her reach.

She listened to Anna's voice tell her story of coming to Angel Creek. Sarah heard the curious questions from the youngest generation wanting to understand how their family came to be.

Sarah thought's drifted again. Soon, the noise of the families faded away and she heard a familiar voice whisper her name, soft and sweet as an angel's wing.

"Sarah?" She heard her name again. She opened her eyes and there, right in front of her, stood her handsome husband, his hand extended to her. "Hello, my darling."

"Quinn?" Her heart pounded in her chest and she couldn't seem to catch her breath. "Is that really you?"

"Yes, Sarah. It's me. Are you ready to go with me? I've missed you so much." His familiar voice caressed her tired and aching soul.

"Oh, yes, Quinn. I'm ready to go. I've missed you too." Sarah reached for his hand and he pulled her from her earthly bonds and into his loving arms for all eternity.

⸺⸺

ABOUT THE AUTHOR

Born and raised in Oklahoma, Peggy McKenzie has been in love with happy endings and second chances of the old west as far back as she can remember. Mesmerized by Miss Kitty and Marshal Dillion made her want to write her own romance stories.

A move to southwest Colorado allows her to write the novels she has always dreamed of writing in the beautiful mountain home she shares with her husband, Jim, and their three fur babies, Augustus McCrae (Gus), Maddie, and Miki (Mickie).

Join her newsletter and fan club @ peggymckenzie.com.

Follow Peggy on social media to learn more about this author and new releases.

MORE BOOKS BY PEGGY MCKENZIE

BRIDES OF THE RIO GRANDE
Grace – Book One
Faith – Book Two
Hope – Book Three
Charity – Book Four
Mary – Book Five (Nov 2019)
Aggie – Book Six (Dec 2019)
Olivia's Obligation

LANGLEY'S LEGACY SERIES
Finn's Fortune – Book One – Kathleen Ball
Patrick's Proposal – Book Two – Hildie McQueen
Donovan's Deceit – Book Three – Kathy Shaw
Aidan's Arrangement – Book Four – Peggy McKenzie
Heath's Homecoming – Book Five – Merry Farmer
Colin's Challenge – Book Six – Sylvia McDaniel

THE END

Made in the USA
Columbia, SC
20 January 2020